Searching For Zen
A Tale Of Divine Destiny

Albert T. Franklin

Dedication

To everyone who has loved and helped me in this journey called life. Too many to count here but know that I have not forgotten any of you.

And also to the ones who always felt they had a story to tell but never the time to tell it.

Acknowledgment

Thank you to my dear wife who takes such great care of me.

My family whose love and support have let me live a life I am proud of.

Thanks, Valisha for inspiring me to just do it.

Contents

About The Author

The Author spent his twenties roaming as much of the earth as he could, started a business with a borrowed van and a credit card with a $2500 limit at age 33, and built it to be a million-dollar-a-year company. Married in 2009 and enjoys traveling with his wife and learning to enjoy the moment.

Preface

This is a simple story of someone who was lonely and lost but he fought to find a family and love. And really aren't we all fighting the same battle?

Introduction

The world today feels like it is coming apart, division and hate seem to be more prevalent than ever before. It is easy to feel lost and lonely when the world is in such chaos. This book narrates a similar journey of a man who felt the same, lost and lonely, and tracks how he travels the world, fighting against all odds to find himself a place where he belongs. Although it is just fiction I hope it brings a small respite from whatever worldly troubles that may plague you.

Chapter 1

A dark shadow had covered the earth for some time now, life felt cheap. The powerful ground the masses into the dirt and did everything in their power to keep the population poor and uneducated. The influential control what the masses think and tell them who and what to hate. The constant propagating combined with the prevalent ignorance in the land exacerbated the hardship for all. It seemed as if humanity was headed backward.

God could hear the inhabitants of the earth collectively groan as he looked down on his creation. He concluded that it was time he sent a new champion to see if they could help get humanity back on track.

The All-powerful God then gave one of his trusted angels the task of finding a child with a good heart. Once found he would be titled with the name of Zendaria. If he can prove himself worthy, then he could rule and pull together the masses, making a grand civilization that could help mankind improve itself. But how can one prove itself worthy of handling such an important task? What makes a good person?

The angel searched the earth for a child with a good heart, something unknowable to humans. It is almost impossible for them to distinguish between a good and a bad heart from just looking at someone but not to spirit beings. He was looking in on many, but one caught his attention. His focus was on a baby being born on an island kingdom to the north called Britannia, to a poor single mother. His father sent off to fight for the lord of the land, was killed before seeing his son born. Due to this, the lord took pity on them and allowed them to stay.

The family didn't have much to begin with, but his mother worked hard to keep what she had. His mother had been orphaned at a young age due to illness and never knew love till she met her husband. She was a kind woman with long blonde hair. After her husband died a piece of her broke that was never healed, and she would never remarry. She loved her son, and he was the best part of her life but for reasons unknown to her as he grew up, he started to drift away from her and seemingly everyone else. She would still try to bridge the gap and always show how much she loved him, which he knew even if he couldn't figure out how to express it.

Life continued normally as any other until the boy reached the age of ten. He woke up one morning with a terrible fever that lasted throughout the day into the evening. His mom feared he would not last the night, so she called the local healer. While he was examining the boy, it happened for the first time. All the memories, all the knowledge and wisdom from this man transferred to the boy. He was terrified and confused. His head was spinning. He reached for his mother for comfort and when their hands touched the same thing happened. He saw flashes of a man that looked like him, images of his youth from someone else's eyes.

Not fully understanding what this meant he kept it to himself. Little by little he started collecting people's lives, their stories. It didn't seem to influence anyone else, just him. It changed him, being suddenly filled with so much information and human experience made him wise beyond comprehension. In a matter of weeks, a mere ten-year-old boy gained a collective total of almost 300 years of wisdom and skills.

In a way to process the constant inflow, his mind organized itself. It was like a library; each life was a book stored on a shelf. They are to be pulled out and read from when needed. He could do anything he obtained without having trained for it personally. He knows exactly how to mold a sword from a block of metal like that of the most experienced blacksmith. All this and more were at his disposal. However, he was just ten so he didn't understand yet how best to use this or a bigger meaning might be.

The following winter his mother's health began to decline. It was a very cold winter that seemed to last forever and the whole earth felt like it had frozen solid. The whipping freezing winds always came up the valley to their small worn-out house at the top of a large hill next to a deep forest. He tried to heal her by means of what he learned from the healer, yet nothing worked. The villagers helped in any way they could so when they saw how she had only gotten worse they tried to remove him from seeing the pain of losing his mother. Something was telling him if he just touched her again, he could heal her. As he raced to get back to her side, the neighbor's wife had come out and said she had passed away. Pushing past everyone he desperately ran to touch his mother. When he did, the earth shook, snow flew off the roof and there was a blast of air coming from inside the house. With tears in his eyes, he looked up and his mother opened her eyes and smiled at him. By some miracle, he had brought her back and this scared his neighbors. Everyone kept their distance from then on for fear he was possessed by some evil.

This caused him to stop connecting with actual humans in his life which led to him doubting himself. The boy didn't know who he was. The stigma he carried made him unsure if he was a good person. Everyone but his mom was afraid of him.

It took a few days until his mom fully recovered, so the boy started venturing out into the woods around his house. He spent much of his time in solitude. He knew what the villagers thought of him, so he stayed away focusing on his healing powers. It was a way to make him stronger.

When life finally felt like it returned to normal, spring had arrived. This also meant that three seasons had now passed by without them having been able to pay any taxes. That fact did not go unnoticed, and soon they received a visit from the landowner Lord Hatt. The mother had been sick for so long they barely had enough to survive let alone be able to pay tribute.

Lord Hatt personally made the trip enraged that he had not received any money for so long. He had allowed them to stay when there was no man to care for them so in his mind, they should be repaying his kindness in plenty. The mother begged for forgiveness on her knees and promised to pay what was owed. But the Lord was in no mood to listen. Taking insult to this response, a hand harshly hit the woman's face forcing her to fall to the ground facefirst.

When the lord hit his mother for not having anything, the boy stepped between his mother and her assailant with a handful of coins. He handed them over and said that should pay for a few years. The lord thought the boy must have stolen the money. He lurched toward the boy with the intent to teach him a lesson for his disrespect. Shoving the boy to the ground and as he went to kick him the boy recoiled, his body covering his head with his hands in anticipation of pain. But the blow never came.

He opened his eyes slowly and saw everything stood still. The wind was still, all was quiet, and everyone seemed to be frozen where they stood. Only he could move around. This caused anxious excitement in the boy. Despite the confusion in his mind, his body got up and ran away. The very next moment, all the surroundings came alive again. A foot swung hard at the empty air causing the body to fall heavy on the ground. The lord was bewildered, as well as the others, as to how the child vanished in a mere second.

The boy stayed in the woods for a while, but he had no idea how or why that phenomenon happened. His mind searched for answers as to why this was happening to him. In all the information he had nothing came close to what others experienced or saw. He had no one to confide in and it just made him feel utterly alone in this world. He knew his mother loved him, but she would never truly be able to understand what he was going through. He thought it would be best to protect her by staying quiet.

He walked deeper into the woods contemplating all that had transpired in his brief time on this earth. He came across another what seemed like a child and immediately hid behind some bushes. He didn't want to be caught by any of the villagers in fear of how they may treat him.

"I can hear you," the stranger spoke to him, turning around to reveal someone much older.

"What do you think you're doing over there? You're not very good at surprise attacking people," said the stranger loudly.

The boy stood up revealing himself. "I'm sorry. I didn't know you were out here. Usually, I'm the only one in these woods."

"Well humans are afraid of this forest, and I like it that way! That means I don't have to put up with you lot," the small man shot back.

"Why are you here?" the boy asked.

"What kind of question is that? I live here, of course. My name is Helgat."

The boy stood there quietly staring.

"Human children should not be out here alone. There are dark things in this Forrest." Helgat warned.

"Why do you live out here then." the boy asked curiously.

Helgat gave a puzzled look. "I'm a Dwarf that has lived here for 200 years, I'll have you know. It was a much nicer place before the humans showed up and took over the land."

"I'm sorry." The child apologized seemingly for an entire race as if he, himself, was the trespasser. The boy had never met someone besides a human.

"You should be safe at home." Helgat continued. He could tell this boy was different. Not only because he wasn't rude but there was something more to him.

The boy didn't say anything, just looked at him.

"Have you eaten anything, boy?"

The boy shook his head.

"Come to my house. It is right over there. You should fit just fine." Helgat told him.

The cracking of the fire was the only noise as the soup was cooked. Helgat sat a bowl down in front of his guest for the first time in a long time to eat first.

"Go ahead you can eat, it's ok."

The boy greedily went at the soup. The saltiness lingered on his tongue, but the heat warmed his belly and he enjoyed each bite. Helgat made a bowl for himself and sat down with him. "So why aren't you with your own kind?"

"They don't like me," responded the boy shyly.

"Huh, well they don't like me either," Helgat said. He paused for a moment but feeling a type of kindred spirit he continued.

"You know this forest used to be full of dwarfs, hundreds of us. We were happy or at least that's the way I like to remember it. That was until humans showed up. Whether by attacking us or plaguing us with their diseases our clans drastically declined." Helgat spoke solemnly staring off into the distance as he held the spoon of soup to his mouth.

"Why don't they like a harmless child like you?"

The boy smirked but said nothing. He showed the dwarf his empty hands and then closed them. When he opened them, there was gold in each hand. Helgat was astonished.

"Do it again!" Helgat urged with childlike excitement. He bit the gold piece in disbelief that it was real.

The boy consented and demonstrated again. Helgat let out a hearty laugh enjoying the show. The atmosphere was contagious. The Dwarfs' joy made the boy happy and in turn, he showed off again. It was the first time he was able to make someone laugh with his ability.

"I will give this to you as a gift for being so nice to me." The boy offered.

Helgat felt the boy's sadness in his words. He came over to the boy and put his arm around him.

"It's not wrong to be sad but you shouldn't let it consume you. If those humans don't like you because you're different, they are stupid. A boy that is a gold fountain, and they don't like it? HA!" Helgat exclaimed.

"They just don't realize how special you are. You wait until you get older and go find people who do see it. They are out there. I hate humans and even I have found some over the years to be tolerable. Even met a few nice like you. Just don't let it stop you from looking for those special ones out there. It's when you stop looking that is when you lose." Helgat told him.

The boy said very little but listened intently to Helgat talk to him throughout the evening. He ended up staying the night and leaving early the next morning. It wasn't the last time he saw Helgat. It was his first real acquaintance he had and cherished that. From time to time, he would visit, giving him gold for some soup and listening to a new story. He never once touched Helgat for the fact that it made him feel normal. He learned about a person through regular communication and the thrill of not knowing something.

Chapter 2

Amongst the forest, there was a small grassy hill that overlooked a pond. A large rock jutted up providing a perfectly secluded place for the boy to rest when he ventured through the woods. One night he was awakened by a brightness as if the sun had flashed in his face. It was a figure walking towards him calling out his name. The young boy responded although frightened.

"Here I am. What is it you want?" he muttered in a shaky voice.

The figure introduced himself as a Guide and said that his purpose was to help him understand his abilities. He explained that every couple hundred years God sends someone to be a champion for the people. This is needed to tilt humanity into a prosperous time. The guide was the one charged with finding the boy. He searched the world for a time and his journey had led him to the child in front of him.

He went on to explain what the boys' powers are in detail. The first one is when he touches anyone's skin, he will take all their memories, skills, and wisdom. That will help give him a greater understanding of people and what makes them do and say things. The next power is he can control matter, he cannot bring anything to life that is only for the True God, but he can make anything come into existence even a human body. The boy asks how he brought his mom back. The figure told him she had not died yet but almost was, if he had been a couple more seconds late, she would have been gone.

His last power was the ability to stop time. At the moment he can only activate it for a few seconds but as he grows in strength, he will be able to weld time like someone wields a sword. The figure then tells him he is the next Zendaria and from that moment the boy takes the name of Zen. After helping the boy understand what he could do, he then took time to explain what was expected of him. He would have to get stronger and wiser, and he would go on a great quest, to find a group of people and artifacts that would help him grow and be ready for what the Guide called the final test.

He had but one warning, he must hide these powers as not all humans will understand. As he grows in strength he then will need to be worried about attracting spirit beings' attention.

"If you draw their ire the consequences are on you," the Guide warns.

After that night the boy had a renewed purpose and felt as if he understood what to do. He started seeking people out like the blacksmiths, great swordsmen healers, and priests. Taking their knowledge, skills, and life experience made him the wise man in the kingdom. But he would hide it in an attempt to be a normal 12-year-old boy. Also, the boy went to talk to the priest who served a congregation in the village nearby where Zen, as the boy was now to be called, lived. Since God had picked him, he felt he needed to know as much as he could about him, touch the priest, and make friends with him so he could learn and understand about faith. The elderly Priest, Memon, heard rumors concerning the boy and how he was an outcast in the area. He was kind to the boy in an effort to show that not all people are the same. He was fascinated with how much knowledge the boy possessed. Zen could seemingly understand Latin even though he never went to school. Instead of being intimidated, he decided to reach out and guide the boy.

While on his way to visit someone, Memon heard a loud commotion and walked over to see what the disturbance was. Some boys were throwing rocks at Zen.

"Stop, or I will make you!" Zen yelled.

At that, a large bear came running out of the woods to the space between Zen and the other boys. The bear lunged at the boys, swiping viciously at them but soon froze. Zen was standing behind it with eyes closed and arm outstretched in a closed fist. The motion he made was like he was tossing a twig to the wind. The animal was thrown back into the woods. The boys ran off crying only to further expand the rumors about Zen's supposedly demonic powers.

Memon reasoned if the boy was evil, would he save the tormentors who hit him with rocks? Although this boy was different maybe he could foster the good in him.

There was a conversation that always stood out to Zen and he pondered on it often. Memon asked him what the most powerful force in the world was. Zen was unsure so the priest taught him about God's holy spirit.

"Think of it this way, His arms and hands are so mighty nothing can stand in the way of what God wants done."

Then he went on to relay to the boy something that would always stay with him the holy writing that said

11

From Holy Writings, "If you have faith the size of a small seed, you will say to this mountain, 'Move from here to there,' and it will move; and nothing will be impossible for you."

Zen would listen intently to the aged priest and ponder on these things.

Even though he had all this experience in him and an outlet from the priest and his dwarf friend in the woods. This was still very difficult for him to process. Since he was so young his powers made it all the harder for him to know who he was and what he was about. This sort of made him introverted as with his limited human connection, it was hard to balance this himself, and struggled to connect with the ones around him.

At first, he took skills from great hunters and farmers but once he realized he could materialize meat, flour, money, and clothes the old skills meant less. It was more beneficial to hone these new skills. He realized he needed to take care of his mother and neighbors to make sure they had enough but not too much that it would raise suspicion. By the age of 16, he learned all he could in his village and outlying towns he had already gathered the collective human experiences of more than 700 years by then.

One night Zen decided to go to the next largest town where the castle of the local royalty resided. He thought a king now must hold a life of experiences that would surely help him grow. But how wrong he was for growth is not what he got from the King's experiences. He told his mom his plan and left the next day. She didn't want him to go but he seemed determined and she didn't stand in his way. He told her he would be back before the harvest season was over.

Chapter 3

One day, as the King rode down the street on his horse, Zen reached out and touched a small part of his leg that was exposed. For the first time he felt the man murdering innocent men, women, and children, he felt him rape young ones. He was repulsed and stood there in the street even after the crowd had gone away horrified of what now was in his mind. He wished there was a way to forget but all those experiences like all the others are burnt into his mind.

The next few people he touches also happen to be very bad and from that moment on he realized he needed to start being careful who he touches and started wearing gloves and full sleeve hooded coats from then on. He was right, he was hoping to learn from the city, but he learned how cruel humans are greedy and selfish.

After a very disappointing day, Zen accidentally bumped into a man, and he saw that this man had a young woman and man tied up in his horse barn and was doing terrible things to them. He felt like he must do something and as night fell, he went up to the barn door and peaked in. He saw a small fire and heard the man saying something to the tied-up man and slapping him. He yelled at him to do something, but Zen couldn't make it out and before he even had the chance to try, the man's wife came up behind Zen.

"what do we have here?" she leered pressing a pitchfork against Zen's back.

Then she pushed him into the barn. Hearing them enter the man turned around and Zen saw that he had his pants down. "What is this?" he barked. The wife said "I got you a new toy." poking at Zen with the pitchfork. He could now see the other two who were tied up. Zen said calmly, "If you let all three of us go no one will get hurt." The man laughed an eerie laugh that could send goosebumps down one's spine and started walking towards Zen. "No! We want the hurt."

But at that very moment, Zen used his powers to make the wife's organs stop working and she died instantly, dropping to the floor. Zen turned his hands up and closed his one fist and then smacked them together and the femur bones in his legs broke and burst out of the skin and the man dropped screaming. Then he held his hand out flat palm up and closed his fist tight and the man's tongue ripped out of his mouth.

Zen then ran and went to untie the two captives, but they were terrified and thought he was going to hurt them too, and would not stop screaming. He just made the ropes disappear from a distance and told them to run. Seeing their reactions to him, confused Zen greatly since he was there to help them. And he started to wonder.

Was he the monster everyone thought he was? Was he saving people or just hurting them, he just wasn't sure anymore. The terrified look in those two eyes even though he was saving them would always stick with him.

When he first arrived, he noticed a beautiful older woman who served drinks at the inn he was staying at. Over time the women noticed him and started to give him attention. After a couple more months she really started to charm him, and Zen liked the attention. Finally, she asked him to come home with her and Zen agreed but when they were about to leave the inn, he touched her. He saw that she had conspired to kill him with the man she lived with and take his stuff as he had been staying at the inn for a long time and figured he had a lot of money. This also made Zen think that a lot of people were just bad and really made it harder to trust and connect with actual humans around him and not just their experiences. This really made the loneliness set in, he didn't feel close to anyone and the silence in his life was so deafening it was becoming harder to focus on his thoughts.

Right after that happened, he left the city and went back to his mother.

On the way home he found himself deep in the woods on the road, but it was almost dark, and he thought he should find a place to lie down. About the same time, several young poor dirty men and boys came up over a hill and came down and surrounded Zen.

"Well would you look at this boy?, This bloke walking all alone in our space, and he doesn't even have a weapon on him, the disrespect," the leader said.

"It's like no one fears us anymore boys and we can't have that now, can we?" He added.

"No," they all yell together.

Zen said, "I assure you I have nothing of value."

"That coat is nice," the leader remarked.

The group closed the circle a little more.

Zen said, "I will give you two warnings but the third will be the last you ever get."

They all laughed.

Zen said, "Pull out your swords let's see what you got."

Two of the bigger boys grabbed them and started to pull them out of their belts when Zen put his hand up and made a fist then struck to his left, The swords became snakes and turned and bit the boys holding them and they screamed and ran off dropping the snakes.

The leader now, who was scared but felt challenged yelled go get him and Zen again made some hand gestures and instantly they were all naked. This really freaked them out and it turned out they weren't all boys, but all ran back over the hill and into the woods.

Zen knew they were just poor uneducated orphans but were there any good people left in the world, he was beginning to think not. However, he was happy with himself that no one really got badly hurt this time.

Even though he was many miles away from his mother, he could still feel her and made sure she had everything she needed even if he was nowhere around. After those experiences, he wanted to be alone and focused on using his power to stop time and spent most of his time deep in the woods. He got to the point he could stop it for hours and he could even open a void and stay there and think and go over the experiences he had taken in.

There was no mage or wizard in his area no men of great power so he didn't know where he would stand with others who might have power, he just kept training. When he turned 18 the spirit figure came back and told him it was time for him to go. "You will collect five people who will join your party and help you grow and become stronger. Together you with your five companions will have to go and get different relics that will help you in your test. Your quest will lead you to the east where you will undergo a final test in which either you will die or ascend to another level."

The boy asked "What happened to other ones like me? "

"Some made it, some didn't, some helped steer mankind to a better path, and some took them down a darker one. The last one was the strongest there ever was! However, his people left him as he went through some of the smaller tests on the way, as will you by the way, because they grew fearful of his powers. By the time came for his final test he was all alone, and he was completely destroyed by it."

"How can I avoid that?" asked the boy.

"You can't! All you can do is search and find what will help you to be stronger, wiser, smarter, and hope it is enough."

"What should I call you?" he asked

"Just call me the guide." The bright figure replied. "Now head to the southern city where you will meet the first person who will join you and then cross the channel and go to one of the largest cities in the world where you will find number two."

"How will I know it's them? How will we become friends and trust each other?" He asked.

"When they come you will know and sometimes you need to trust first so friendship comes," the guide responded and disappeared leaving Zen with a gazillion questions racing through his head. But he shoved them aside, packed his things, and said goodbye to his mother. He told her he loved her but had to go, and although she loved the boy, she knew that it might be best for him. Here, he was an outcast, termed as a strange boy compared with the others in the neighborhood. He was a boy who seemingly could do everything but had no friends, no girlfriend, and was very quiet and not like the other boys his age. When he was going, she feared she would never see him again but she didn't stand in his way.

Chapter 4

So, he set off for the southern city, and as he was walking, he realized he didn't need anything, if he wanted to stay at an inn he could make money, if there was nothing, he could make something to eat. He didn't need a change of clothes he could just make them new each day. This made the journey so much easier and fun. He still was careful now who he touched but if there was someone, he thought he could learn from he would manage to touch them. While he enjoyed walking during the day and thinking of his new grand adventure, at nighttime, he just mostly felt alone.

About halfway through a small village towards the outskirts, he saw a small dirty boy standing in a corner of the road that leads southward to village Abbey.

The boy asked as Zen got closer.

"Would it be ok if I walked with you for a while, it is not safe to walk alone this way."

"Sure," said Zen.

At first, they both are quiet, but the little boy starts pointing and telling him about the area.

Zen then said, "May I ask you a question?"

"Yes, sir," the boy said.

"What happened to your leg?" Zen asked.

"Oh, I was born with this sir, You see I heard the neighbors saying that I must have sinned against God, and he punished me this way. I'm not sure what I did but I'm really sorry I did it. I wish I could make it up to him, but I guess it was a pretty bad sin for him to do this" the boy said.

"I see," said Zen.

His dirty worn pants covered the leg, but he walked very oddly, and it looked painful.

"I hope someday I maybe could make him proud of me and maybe he rewards me with good legs, and I could run," the boy said getting a big smile on his face.

"What is your name?" Zen asked taking off his gloves.

The boy smiled even bigger and said "Otto sir, I'm Otto"

"My name is Zen."

But inside he didn't want to ask more because he didn't want to do something that was just going to terrify him or his family like everyone else.

The boy said, "You know no one ever asked me my name before."

"Is that so?" Zen said.

Otto then went on to tell a story about his two sisters and how sweet they are and other stuff that is very important when you're six or seven.

Otto looks up at Zen and says "Can I tell you a secret, I don't want to get in trouble."

Zen said, "I promise your secret is safe with me."

I went to the market to steal food. He looked down and was ashamed.

"Did you?" Zen asks

He looked up with a smile no, no I didn't take anything.

"Why not?" Zen asked.

"A little while ago my family was coming home from church, but we decided to take a faster way home through the woods but there were bad men there. They tied me and my sisters to a tree and they beat my dad up really bad, and they kept hurting my mom because she kept screaming and I wanted to help her, but I couldn't get free, and that all made me very sad."

"Why did that make you not take food?" Zen asked.

"I didn't want to make someone else feel like that" Otto replied.

"I see," Zen said.

"Why did you need food?" Zen asked.

"My dad is a good dad and a very, very hard worker he is not a Scobberlotcher at all sir. He worked for Lord Whitgift. He has not been mean to us at all, he liked my dad, and he said he was a hard worker. He was working in his stable and the son came flying in on his horse, it was out of control and kicking everywhere and it ended up kicking my dad in the chest," Otto said matter-of-factly.

"I heard grown-up saying he won't get any better and he is in a lot of pain, but he tries not to moan too much," the boy continued.

"I asked the healer in town if he could come and see him, but he said we don't have money so he is not coming," Otto said.

Zen was listening quietly the whole time even though his heart went out for this kid. He didn't want to terrify them any more than they already were.

For a bit, they were both quiet but Zen was watching Otto, but he seemed to be working something out in his head.

Otto then said "OK my house is over there, Thank you for walking with me," and he cut off the road and limped down a small dirt trail.

He got about ten or twelve steps and Zen yelled out Otto's name.

"Yes," the boy said turning around.

Zen took a deep breath and said, "I -ummm, I know a little about healing.." he stammered trying to sound confident. "I mean I did it back home a little I mean I know some. Maybe I could look at your dad for you," Zen said feeling like an idiot and trying to figure out how was he not going to scare them.

"Yes, oh please thank you Zen" and the boy waved his arm to come this way, "Oh! thank you."

When they got to the house the boy opened the door and proclaimed his friend Zen was here and he was a healer. His mother worried and thought maybe he was a bad person taking advantage of her sweet son.

When Otto turns he sees Zen wearing a very large backpack that he didn't remember having before.

Zen reached out his hand to greet the mother "Hello I'm Zen," and took her hand and kissed it as that is what they did in polite society, but this made her blush, and no one had ever done that before.

With that, he saw what those bad men had done, Otto mentioned, and all the violence and abuse she had lived through, but she then met a man who everyone looked down on because he was small and scrawny, but he treated her well and loved her and tried to be a good dad and a hard worker.

Before she could say anything, Otto said "Her name is Gertrude and those are my twin sisters" and upon mention two small dirty girls with hair all over came out of a back room. They looked like they had not eaten in weeks.

Then Otto ran over and said "This is my dad," putting his hand on his stomach. He was a small wiry man but looked sturdy besides the extremely large bruises on his chest and his extremely labored breathing.

Gertrude looks at Zen and for a second just hopes for good then expecting bad.

Zen then takes his backpack off and puts it on the table and says to everyone.

"Today Otto did a bad thing and went to town to steal food," and his mom was terrified that this was about to get really bad.

"But then he decided to do something great," Zen said.

Otto said, "What was that?"

"He decided to be good," Zen said with a smile.

23

"Nowadays good very rarely ever gets rewarded but this time your son found an angel of God. I was sent here to bless this whole family because Otto made God proud" he said as he reached out and put his hand on Otto's head.

It bothered Zen to lie but this was the only way they might not be afraid.

Everyone was shocked, especially Otto as his eyes grew wide.

Zen then opened the backpack and there were all sorts of salted meats and vegetables. Then Zen put his hand down on the table and when he picked it up there were 5 large gold coins, more than this family would see in a lifetime.

Then he went over to the dad and sat down and put his hand on his chest and the entire bed bucked up and down. Then the bruises went away, and his breathing got much better.

Then he asked the girls to come to him and he hugged them and removed their deficiencies and even gave them a little body fat to live off. He went over to Mom, put his hand on her shoulder, and said "I'm sorry the scars inside won't heal but the ones outside will."

Then he turned and said "Now it's your turn, Otto"

"Mine," Otto said.

"Come over here" Otto came and sat on a chair with a huge smile and Zen smiled at the boy and said, "You have made him proud." He held his leg and healed it and a few other things the boy didn't even know. After that, Otto hugged Zen tightly and proudly showed his mom and sisters his new leg.

Zen watched as the kids sang and danced around and Otto was running everywhere as fast as he could. By then his father was strong enough to sit up.

Zen turns to them and says" I will be on my way." He then warned their neighbors might not understand what happened here, maybe take the money and start someplace else but it was up to them, and he turned to open the door.

"Please wait, please eat with us and stay the night. Don't sleep in the cold, let us try to repay you," Gertrude asked.

He decided to stay and watch this family just be happy together maybe just for tonight, but at least they got that one night.

The downside was Zen couldn't help thinking that if he told them the truth, they would be terrified of him. However, with a lie, they loved it and even felt honored. It was confusing to process for Zen and even though they didn't mean to, the incident made Zen feel more distant from everyone else and more alone.

The next morning, he was gone before any of them woke up.

Chapter 5

Finally, he made it to the southern city called London, and he spent the first few days wandering the city when he overheard that a great mage was coming to the city to see the king's wizard. He thought that would be amazing, are they like me he wondered.

He went to the square where the mage would show the people his power and ask his gods for blessing. It didn't take long for the boy to realize that this man had no real power. That was more disappointing than he had thought but maybe the wizard had true power and surely must be since it is considered a step higher than mage.

So, he followed the mage to the wizards' dwelling; they both talked outside and made a great show to the people. After they went inside the boy decided to try to dress as a servant and touch them both. As he was serving dinner at the party, he touched each person. All fakes, he thought. They could play with potions or sleight of hand, and some could do small feats of magic but nothing worth taking notice of. Then as he was about to leave, he bumped into and touched a younger man no older than 20 and realized he had something. It was very hard for Zen, but he decided he must trust his instincts and try to reach out to this one and see what would happen.

Since he was touching people so fast, he couldn't keep up with all their lives at once. He would need a bit of time to process but the boy had power. So, he waited for the boy outside, when he finally came out, he started to approach him, and the boy said "If you're looking for a companion I'm not interested." Zen not knowing what to say stammer at the response. "No, no, listen what if I told you that you are stronger than everyone in that room tonight."

"What!" The other boy said, "That was mage Hendron and the great wizard Magnel who served the king for 30 years."

"All fakes!" Zen exclaimed. "Let me buy you a drink and I will explain. What's your name?" Zen asked. "Duncan" he responded. Now Duncan was not one to turn down free booze, so they went. Zen had never told anyone besides the Guide about his real self, so it was very hard to get started and know what to say but the alcohol helped loosen him up. Zen figured he just started from the beginning and told him everything and went for broke.

Zen told him his story which Duncan thought was a great tale but was a complete lie. Zen said "So I will prove it to you" and made two small coins appear for the drinks. Sleight of hand Duncan responded; "Any trickster could do that."

He then would really have to prove it to him. So he started by telling Duncan things about his life and his power. "You can not only understand any language you hear but can also transfer that ability to another person."

Duncan was shocked and had no words. Is this guy for real, he has never told anyone about his abilities how could this stranger know?

"Now do you believe me?" asks Zen.

Duncan said, "I've never told anyone about that."

Zen then says "I know that is why I knew it would help you realize you're the first person to join me on my quest East."

Duncan is of average height and very outgoing and witty, he came from a large family, and he was the second youngest. His father was a Taylor in the city and afforded them a decent life. This allowed Duncan to be free and try to find his own way in life. He always loved adventure stories as a child and had always dreamed of going on one himself. He found early in life he had special abilities but always kept them to himself in fear of others like his parents. He had thought these abilities would help him if he got a chance to travel.

They would spend the rest of the night talking and planning for what seemed like a great journey to Duncan and he had always dreamed of a big adventure since he was young. He would ask all the questions that Zen already figured out on his way there. Duncan then thought I needed to settle my affairs and tell my family I was leaving.

The next few days they became fast friends as Duncan got ready and on the last night, Duncan said he was taking Zen someplace special. As they went into the establishment, they took a small table in the back and then a parade of women came out of the back after a little while. Zen looked and said "What is this place?"

"What do you mean, man you are a country kid," laughs Duncan. "You pick one of these women and you go into a room in the back and have some adult fun."

Zen said abruptly, "I cannot do this Duncan; these women don't really want to be here they just don't have a choice."

"Of course, they want to be here. They love pleasure but also money" he giggled.

"It's ok Duncan, you can go ahead I'll wait outside for you." Duncan was like wait, wait and he grabbed a very cute young petite blond girl and shoved her gently toward Zen making them touch. Zen slowly watched in his head as her life played out. This sweet, beautiful little thing with such a fiery spirit was being abused and mistreated. He watched her crying and wishing for a better life and that someone would care enough to take her away from all this. Zen looked into her eyes and with a tear running down his cheek he said "I'm sorry Shayari," using her name. She asked how he knew her, but Zen didn't respond. She thought, "Can you read my mind?"

Zen looked at Duncan and Duncan could tell something was wrong, so he grabbed Zen and left. "Wait," exclaimed Zen. "What? Now you want to go in? Make up your damn mind!" Duncan said exasperated.

"No, we need to take her and let her go home back to the countryside. She is dying inside Duncan we must do something."

Duncan was confused but also wondering about his friend.

Zen went back in, grabbed her, and whispered, "I know you are praying for a change. Meet me at the town square at dawn and I will help you."

"She will never show, she probably thinks you are some sort of creep," said Duncan as they walked away from the brothel.

29

The next morning after the boys were ready to go, they first went to the square where the small woman was already waiting for them. She said, "I started to think you would not actually show."

Then as all three started to leave the city, Duncan asked her "Why did you show up this morning?"

Shayari then explained that after Zen spoke to her, she told her friend she was sick and ran to get her things and had been there the whole night hoping they would come.

With amazement, Duncan said, "What did he say to you?"

She said "He told me a prayer I have been saying every night ever since I got stuck in this situation. My mother taught me that prayer when I was little. No one could know that. So he must be an angel!" Duncan was in total disbelief of all that Zen had done the past few days and he became mesmerized thinking about it as they walked.

On the walk, she told them how she was lured away at a young age with a job offer to help her family back home. However, when she got there the lord forced himself on her and his wife got angry and had her banished from their property, so she ended up at the brothel.

Zen turned to her and said "Forget the past, go live your future. Find the love you are looking for." He said handing her a bag full of gold. "I truly hope you find some happiness."

Looking into the bag and seeing the gold, she looked with sad eyes and said "Can I go with you?"

Zen said, "No, I am sorry, but it is too dangerous." He knew they may not survive, and wanted her to live a long, beautiful life.

"With that money, you can do whatever you want to do, just hide it and only share it with the person who feels like your answered prayer." She shook her head yes and started walking down the path off to the east as the sun rose.

Duncan said, "You're a good man Zen, that was amazing." Zen said nothing as both watched her walk away.

It was while they watched her walk off that Zen had completely won Duncan's admiration, but Zen could not help thinking about what a life with her would have been like.

Duncan then said, "You realize there is nothing this way but the ocean?"

"I know," Zen said. "We need to cross it and go to one of the largest cities on earth."

When they got to the shore the water seemed to go on forever. Duncan was mesmerized by the whole scene. After Zen got them passage to the other side, they boarded one merchant ship and headed for Frankia.

While on the boat Duncan couldn't stop thinking of the young girl and what Zen had done so he came and sat next to Zen, "Can I ask you something?" Zen looking up, "You said you take in all those lives, you know everything. All the private moments … like sex?"

Zen shook his head "Yes, I have never experienced it myself, but I've done it many times through others as that is part and parcel of taking someone's memories."

"I'm not trying to be grossed out but then you know what it felt like for those women, man," Duncan asked. "Yes," Zen said.

"I just look at it like two people giving each other pleasure, whoever might be involved. But I also know how destructive it can be and how terrible and painful. When I touched that young woman yesterday, I saw and felt the emptiness, the loneliness. How could I do the same to her? I don't have the heart for it. I will wait till I find someone who loves me, that way when I touch them, I can feel good" Zen explained.

Duncan sat deep in thought about what his friend was telling him, then said "But you don't mind if I do it right" with a laugh.

"I hold no judgments," said Zen.

"Good" exclaimed Duncan with a laugh.

Not long after that, a huge storm came rolling over the waves out of the east very rapidly and soon the small merchant ship was being thrown all over even the crew was starting to get worried, and they told everyone to tie themselves to the ship. The whole time Duncan just stared at Zen thinking 'Well where was all that magic?'

Zen though was afraid to do things in front of people, he had never gotten a good reception when he did anything when he was young. Then a giant wave came over the back of the boat and crashed down, breaking some of the wood. Everyone screamed but it was muffled by the roar of the waves and rain pouring down. Duncan looked at Zen, made eye contact, and said "Please."

Everyone on the boat was in shock and before others could untie themselves to jump off the now-sinking ship. Zen untied himself and stood up closed his eyes and you could see him tighten his body with his hands by his side then he clenched both fists and with a mighty scream he moved his arm slowly up, but they acted as if he was straining with heavy weights attached to his arms. He fought to raise them up over his head and when he clapped his hands above his head the sea calmed, and the storm dissipated.

Everyone was in shock, and he walked to the back of the boat and put both of his hands on the back of the boat floor and the break in the wood healed up. Duncan could not help but jump up and scream "YES!" As Zen walked back to where he was sitting next to Duncan, Duncan yelled out "THE MASTER OF ELEMENTS everyone!" and everyone clapped thankful to be alive but slightly scared at what they had just witnessed.

Not one word was said by anyone but Duncan and Zen till the boat was tied to the dock.

Zen said "That is why I try not to do things, it scares people,"

Duncan looked him straight in the eyes, "NOT ME!" He replied.

Zen was thankful he had trusted his instincts and reached out to Duncan.

Chapter 6

After they got to the other side, they walked to the city but on the way, Duncan asked Zen "When you did what you did on the boat, I saw you moving your hands around. Is that part of something that helps make it happen?"

Sort of Zen said "Moving my hands really doesn't do anything, but it sort of helps me visualize what I'm trying to do. So maybe just a tool to help me concentrate on the will I'm trying to accomplish if that makes sense."

Duncan listened but didn't totally understand but was still just amazed at what Zen had done in the short time he knew him.

They found an inn near the center of town where they got a room and then went down to get something to eat and Zen tried to figure out what to do next.

"So, we are going to find someone else here, right?" asks Duncan "How will we know who he is?"

"I don't know, I was just told that when it happens, I will know" explains Zen.

A short time later two of the city guards sat at the table next to them. One started telling the other about the Demon of the depths, a creature that lives in the sewers below the city and attacks anyone it encounters. They traded wild tales of the viciousness of such a creature. One man said that it was a vengeful Dwarf whose family had been killed in the city and was now seeking retribution on all the poor souls that found themselves in his lair.

The next man said "No, no you are mistaken, it is a Troll who has lost his mind and is possessed by a demon and comes up out of the sewers at night looking for children not in bed yet" he said with a big laugh.

The third man told a tale of a painter who lost his love and now lives in the sewers but comes up at night to kill young girls walking about alone.

Zen looked at Duncan and said, "I think I know where I need to be."

"Do you want me to come along?"

"No, it's ok I'm not sure what dangers await. It's better that I go alone for now," Zen said knowing Duncan was more of a lover than a fighter.

Zen then made his way to the sewers and walked in. He then took his hand resting on top of each other then one circled the other and ended in a joined position. With that gesture, a halo of light went around him lighting the tunnels up like the sun was shining in. He started hearing something in the distance and it was following him, so he walked slower. Zen spoke, "I know you're there it is okay I will not hurt you." Something about this creature seemed to be calling Zen somehow even though it made no noise.

The creature came out of the dark and Zen had never seen something so deformed, so dirty, so hideous in his whole life. The creature mutters a few words, but his mouth is so deformed you can't make anything out. He had and had open sores with puss and blood draining from parts of his head. His one leg was longer than the other but the smaller one moved in a way that seemed like it was badly broken and healed poorly. Every breath seemed to bring nothing but pain to this poor creature's existence.

Zen pondered out loud, "You're no troll or Dwarf or even some weird painter."

He came closer to it and reached out his hand but instead of attacking, the thing just stood there. It sounded like it was crying or very least moaning crying-type sounds. Figuring it must be able to hear Zen asked if he could touch him and slowly reached out.

When he made contact Zen burst into tears and started weeping uncontrollably because what broke his heart the most was the creature was intelligent and could think and feel it all. He sat there for a long time next to the creature as both stayed silent. Then said, "Do you want me to heal you or kill you if you think that is the mercy you need?" Zen asked.

After asking the question Zen touched him again to understand the answer.

The minute he made contact the halo of light went out with a huge boom and a gust of air blew through the sewers chasing out the rats and creatures of all sizes out of the sewer. Zen sat there touching him for a long time when finally, he turned his light back on and there lay a very tall man. He was covered with dark hair and his body was like it was carved out of marble. As he gained consciousness, he tried to speak but no words came out, just gasps and squeaks. "Don't speak, friend, you need time for your mind to get used to your new body," Zen said.

Not saying a word, he followed Zen back to the inn in the very early morning hours. Zen had made him some simple clothes in the sewer, and both came out very dirty. Duncan opened the door as Zen knocked and stared at the very large human behind him. "Duncan, I need you to use your power on him. Help him know our language and how to speak it," Zen requested.

For the next few hours, Duncan hovered over the man with his fingers rubbing his temples. Then he finally sat down, "Did it work?" Zen asked.

"I think so but his mind is confused so he needs some time to work it out, I think," Duncan said in a puzzled way.

Zen told the man to get some sleep and he laid down with his feet hanging a few feet over the bed. Duncan looking at it, Zen said "We will get a bigger room tonight."

When they came back up to the room a few hours later the man was sitting up and crying. He was simply overwhelmed that his nightmare had finally ended. It was as if he died and went to heaven. He had spent most of his life alone being chased by humans and beaten or things thrown at him.

"Hey big guy, you, ok?" asked Duncan. "Thank you! Thank you!" he kept repeating the word over and over and eventually fell at Zens' feet crying and thanking him repeatedly. "It's ok my friend. Get up. Are you hungry?"

"Oh yes, I'm starving," he replied.

They took him downstairs and ordered some food and he started crying again. Duncan felt very uncomfortable watching him cry in public. "Why are you crying now big man it's just lunch," said Duncan.

"I have never eaten inside; I've mostly just eaten rats in the past ten years," the big man said between sniffling and bites.

Duncan took a hard swallow, "Wow that is terrible!" he exclaimed. "What's your name?"

The large man said "My name is Catastavous. I don't remember my family name. I was born to one of the few remaining Elven women who supposedly had been bitten by a werewolf during her pregnancy with my father who was an extremely large man with no hair anywhere. I came out utterly deformed and when I was 5, they threw me in the river. Thankfully, an old bum who lived near my family dragged me out and made sure I had some food. He drank a lot but was kind enough not to beat me and let me stay in his home, which was just a dug-out hole near the sewers. That's where I stayed for years till some young men found me and chased me deep into the sewers. I've lived there alone since then."

"How do I know all these words?" a puzzled Catastavous asked.

Duncan said "It is my power to help your brain understand and use a language. I guess I have already proven useful to our quest," slapping Cat on the back and smiling at Zen. "Yes, you did good," said Zen.

Even with Duncan's help, Cat had no sort of education or care. He wasn't dumb but had a lot to learn and was always saying the wrong words for the situation. But the two boys were patient with him.

Duncan then asks "Why is he so big?"

I copied what his father looked like from his memories. "Though his father was not hairy I'm not sure how that happened, maybe from the werewolf" explained Zen

Duncan interjected "Or the mother" and laughed out loud.

"I think we will call you Cat from now on if that is ok," Duncan said

Devouring the food that was brought to him, Cat agreed he liked that. After eating they all sat there as Zen then told Cat the whole story from his start to Duncan to this moment. With Duncan coloring some of the details. Cat sat in amazement; "An angel sent you to find me?" asked Cat

"I guess you can say that" Said Zen, "Would you like to join us?"

Cat again started crying, "I can be your friend" and burst out even more. Duncan put his arm on his shoulder and said, "You have really got to get the crying under control."

"Let him be, he has had a nightmare existence. Knowing that is over will be hard to take for him." Explaining Zen.

After getting a larger room and bed the three of them stayed there for a couple weeks while Cat got used to his new body and got stronger. After that Zen came to the two of them, "We needed to go south to a small village, there we need to find the 1st relic, a small green stone that is in the center of a pendant with ancient words scribed around it in a circle. It belonged to an ancient healer and had powers that only some can wield."

At first, they thought they would get a cart and horse so it would give Cat more time to get stronger. But when they went to get on, Cat jumped straight up on the back of it catapulting the driver and his wife off the front of the cart while their son was about to tie the horse to it. He had never seen a cart before. After being harshly scolded by the older couple and them wagging their fingers at Cat they all decided to walk.

So, they started and explained all the things they saw to Cat so he could know what they were as he had spent most of his life underground and in darkness.

Finally, they got to the small village, but Cat's size made everyone stare at him, he was as tall as two men, one standing on the other one's shoulders. "Why are they staring?" Cat asked sheepishly. Zen told him because he was so tall and beautiful which of course again made Cat cry, but he did so quietly this time.

"Well, that is an improvement," whispered Duncan to Zen. While what Zen said was true it was also the size of Cat muscles, his legs were as thick as trees and his arms and shoulders were massive not to mention he had a very fierce look on his face.

They stopped to get something to eat but Cat was so large he busted out the chair from underneath him and he was very embarrassed. He tried to get up putting his weight on the table and ended up flipping it over with the people sitting on it, sending them and their lunch flying. They just went outside and sat on the grass and ate their lunch and Zen paid for the damage and lost food. It's not that Cat was clumsy; he just never had this body before it will take some time to get used to the two boys consoled him.

Zen approached a man and said, "We are here looking for your healer can you help us find him?" "Yes, of course! He lives near the edge of the town, in a thatched-roof house, with a wooden door. His is the last house that way so you should have no trouble finding it."

After getting the directions they said thanks and went to the edge of town, Cat was about to knock on his door, but Duncan stopped him and said "Enough damage today" and knocked.

Zen explained that he was there for the pendant and would pay any price for it. The healer pulled out an old box, "The pendant is in here, but you can't pull it out" said the healer, "Why?" Zen asked. "It has an old curse on it, and you must have Elven blood in order to be able to remove it."

Smiling Zen said, "I just happen to have the right man for the job."

"Wow!" Duncan said "Cat to the rescue." This made Cat so proud that he could do something for his newfound friends. In his heart, he was determined that he would repay his debt and prove he was worth saving from those sewers.

The healer asked for a lot of gold because he knew the reputation of the piece and its value, but he had never been able to use the pendant anyway so didn't put up much of a fight and gave it to them for a reasonable price.

Zen then asked, "What does the inscription say?" But the healer had no idea, Zen showed it to Duncan, but Duncan said "I must hear the language to understand sorry." A little dejected, Zen put the pendant on, and they left.

"Where to now?" asked Duncan.

41

Chapter 7

"We are headed East to an enchanted forest where there is a haunted lake. There is a silver dagger that is guarded by an evil spirit. We must figure out how to get it."

As they walked Zen walked behind the two and listened to Duncan teach Cat about life, love, and women and Cat just ate it up both laughing and enjoying the walk. Zen said nothing and just listened to Duncan telling mostly tall tales but also deeply emotional ones.

Zen wished he could be as open as them and share his feelings like them, but he still was trying to figure all of that out. With the extra life experiences, he was not sure how to share and explain who he was inside. It made Zen feel the distance between them all, we wanted to close that distance, but he just didn't know how.

After a few days, they finally came upon an old mine shaft that someone put a door on and made into a home. So, Zen knocked on the door and after a bit, the door opened to find a very old grey-bearded Dwarf standing there. "Master Dwarf hello, we are wondering if you could point us to the way to the lake of despair," asks Zen.

"No, no boys. You don't want to go there. That is a bad place and you shouldn't go there," said the dwarf disapprovingly.

Zen then says, "Well if you point out the way we can avoid going there instead of walking straight into the danger."

"Good point," said the Dwarf, "Go straight up this hill through the dark forest but be careful; there are a lot of creatures in there with bad intentions. At the very top is a lake formation but it is actually a filled-in old crater left by a dried-out volcano.

Duncan asked, "Why do they call it the lake of despair?"

"Well, it is said that a long time ago there was a virgin girl who was kidnapped and taken there to be sacrificed. But before being sacrificed was defiled and then killed and dumped into the lake. People say this displeased the Gods and the entire village was wiped out by a plague for the wrong they did the woman and the young woman has haunted that place ever since."

"Thank you Master Dwarf," Zen said and threw him a gold coin.

"Well, thank you, boys. May many blessings be with you," said the Dwarf excitedly.

They decided to camp at the foot of the hill and then started up through the forest at daybreak. They could hear a low moaning as they got closer to the top. After clearing the forest line, the top of the mountain had a small rim of land, and the rest was a very large lake. There was a broken-down stone structure that might have been a house long ago. They looked around but there was nothing and no one to be seen. Duncan said, "Where do you suppose it is?"

"No idea. But I have a feeling we will find out tonight," Duncan said with a tremble in his voice.

Are we going to stay here for the night?" asked Cat.

"Yes. Let's set up camp before it gets dark," said Zen.

43

They set up camp and all were lying in their blankets when the moaning got loud, the lake seemed to be screaming and a faint echo saying "How could you?" kept coming back to them.

The three of them stood up and as they did, a ghost-like face flew right at them, screaming. At the very last moment, Zen pushed Duncan out of the way and she passed through him. Zen stood there for a moment, bewildered, as for the first time he saw the memories of a spirit creature.

He saw the small village she grew up happily in with her family and three younger siblings. He watched as she had a poor but loving home that did their best to just survive. He watched as a band of raiders ransacked her village and was chasing her younger siblings to the shoreline to capture them, She distracted them to help let them get away, but they took her instead. He saw her smile weakly at them as she was tied up and thrown over the side of one of the raiders' horses as she saw her siblings hiding in the bushes. As she tried not to cry while the horse was carrying her up the hill, she saw her village burn and the bodies of all of them lying all over. Watched the raiders sell her to slavers who then sold her to the priests of a different village for a sacrifice.

He saw the stone house was larger and was built behind a large wooden altar where she was tied for days with no food or water. Then the village elders cut her down on a full moon and ripped her clothes off in front of everyone and let the young man violate her in any way but not vaginally as she must remain a virgin for their gods. She was severely cut up from being pushed down into the hard volcanic rock; the poor and extremely dehydrated woman was abused repeatedly as blood poured down her legs and she begged

44

for death. Finally, after a couple of hours, two young men held her beaten and battered body up and the village priest said a prayer and then cut her throat and they threw her into the lake to die.

Maybe because she is a spirit, he watched it all like he was a floating eye instead of being in her own head and memories. The look on her face and the tears falling as he cut her throat struck Zen hard like nothing had ever struck him before. It completely broke his heart even more than what he watched Cat go through. As the face flew back out to the lake and turned to come back to the three Zen yelled her name, "MARY, wait we are here for you!"

The face stopped abruptly.

"I'm so sorry Mary, I saw what you went through, it was wrong" Zen yelled.

"How do you know my name?" asked the face.

"My name is Zen," he called out to her. "I was sent here to help you find peace," he said.

"What do you know of such things, you are just another wicked man," and the face took off with speed and went straight through Zen again. This time he felt her rage, loneliness, and how broken she was inside, he felt it all.

"Mary help me help you. What do you want?" He said desperate to alleviate her pain and bring her peace. The face started screaming again. The sound it made would terrify any man and did scare Duncan and Cat enough to have them hide behind the stone structure. This time as the face came to Zen, he stopped time and took her spirit to the void with him.

There she was, her body in spirit form still screaming and trying to figure out how to move, "My name is Zen. I have brought you here so we can talk," Zen said calmly.

After she finally calmed down, she yelled at him, "Who are you? What sort of trick is this?"

"Do you not want me to call you Mary?" he asked calmly.

"Mary died a long time ago I'm the evil spirit that is left to seek revenge."

"You are not evil, you have rage, yes, but you also have a broken heart and loneliness that is deeper than I have ever felt. You are still Mary."

"You have no idea who I am and what has happened to me," Mary declared. To prove her wrong, Zen told her what he saw in detail, with tears in his eyes, and said it broke his heart as they held her up and she mouthed please as they cut her throat.

She was quiet for a while, "There is nothing you can do for me. That was 300 hundred years ago. Some of us are just destined only for pain," she said sadly. "Please leave me alone, what do you want?"

"I'm here for you," Zen says, "I need the silver dagger and I can grant you a wish if you help me find it."

"I will guide you to it but you must then kill my spirit so I can rest and stop hurting. Can you do that human?" Asks Mary

"What if I could do something else?" asks Zen

"What else is there?" asks Mary

46

"What if I can give you a second chance? You would be mortal again and age and die, but you could live again." Says Zen

"That's impossible. Why you are just wasting my time?" screamed Mary.

Zen went on to tell her his story just like he had told the others up to this moment.

After listening and thinking about it a bit Mary said "I wish I had run into a man like you back then, maybe my life would have been different."

"I'm going to let you out of the void, if you can show me the dagger, I will grant you this if you want it." Says Zen

Mary then said, "You will just trick me and leave me here alone forever, I know it."

"Sometimes you must trust to be rewarded if you do this for me, I promise I will reward your trust."

Zen knew this to be true as he had to trust that his new friends would respect him and so far, had been rewarded with their friendship.

In a blink, they were back, and she was just a face, and that made her start screaming again and fly off. Zen stood there a while waiting to see if she would come back but everything even the water was eerily still and quiet.

Duncan yelled over "She not coming back Zen." Zen looked over and started to walk back toward them when the voice of the lake said "I will trust you human, please don't let me down like all the others I have ever known."

The spirit rested over the small rim around the lake by the stone structure they threw the silver dagger into the water with me. Look in the water around here and you will find what you want.

Zen put his hands in the water and feeling around, he felt as if the metal was calling to him and helped guide his hand into the volcanic rock and sand till, he picked up an exquisite silver dagger that glistened in the campfire light still going.

"What now human?" yelled the face.

"Come to me, wrap yourself around me, and give me some time."

As it did, the ground started to pick up and swirl around him. After a bit, the spirit felt something and screamed one last time, "Please don't ..."

The stuff swirling in the air all dropped to the ground and everything was very quiet. Then Zen struggled to walk to the stone structure, sat in front of it, and looked as if he was asleep. Cat looked at Duncan and said, "What should we do?"

"I don't know did this happen when he was with you?" asked Duncan.

"I don't remember," said Cat.

They both started walking toward Zen when he said out of a dead sleep, "Please don't come over here stay there for now."

Neither asked any questions, they just sat down and looked around and up at the stars.

After a while dawn broke and the sunrise was amazing from the top of the volcano.

Zen then said "You can come out, and see the sun rise" The two men looked at each other puzzled because they had just been sitting right there. Then a long slender hand reached out of the structure and a stunningly beautiful brunette woman came out in a simple white dress. She stood there mesmerized by the colors of the sunrise.

She muttered some words, but they were not understandable. Zen looked at Duncan, "Your turn."

Duncan walks toward the girl but realizes she is not ready for anyone to touch her, so he does his best from a few feet away. After a little while, she says, "Is this real? It is impossible! Am I dreaming?"

Zen said, "Come and watch the first sunrise of your second life." She stood there touching her arms and feeling her body and watching the man who gave her a second chance at life, standing in the sunrise.

After a bit Zen makes a few fish appear at the water edge where he grabs them and smokes them over the fire. Giving some to all, he also reached out to Mary and gave her the food touching her fingers slightly. This time he felt all her memories and he started to tear up.

Zen then said to Mary, "What I have done won't last forever, you have 100 yrs. starting from this morning. You can die before that but there is no way to live beyond it. Use your time wisely and I hope you finally find happiness." For a long time, Mary said nothing just watched the men eating the food and talking.

"I forgot how good food tasted, it was delicious," says Mary out of the blue.

"Yes, I've never eaten as well as I have with these two," agreed Cat wholeheartedly.

Then Duncan and Cat started telling Mary about their journey and what happened to them both and all the tales they could think of, and she sat there eating the fish and just listening and smiling.

Zen just watched and took it all in and wished he was more like them. After a while, they all lay down and slept a while. At first, Mary's dreams were terrible reminding her of what had happened but then she started dreaming about the beautiful man who saved her and cared. It was the best dream she had ever had.

After getting up Duncan said, "Where to next?"

They were all gathering the few things they had, and Mary was sort of just standing there looking down and kicking something with her foot. Zen asked, "Mary what will you do?"

Mary said, "Everyone I ever knew has been dead for centuries, can I come with you all?"

Zen said, "We would love to have you join us."

Cat then hugged her and squealed, "Alright baby sister!" and she smiled in the embrace.

Zen had after all made both of their bodies, so their being siblings made sense.

This sort of stunned Duncan remembering what Zen had said to the other girl before about joining us but then thought maybe she was supposed to join the group.

Chapter 8

"We must go north toward the old Elven kingdoms. There is a bracelet there I need to acquire," Zen explained. "After that, we will head south, towards the ocean."

"The ocean?" asked Mary. "I've never seen it."

"It is amazing!" exclaimed Duncan as they all started walking again. "I had never seen it till we took a boat across it earlier."

"If we are going on a long journey why don't we have more than some rolled-up blankets." inquired a very confused Mary.

"We have all we need," said Zen. Duncan and Cat started telling her all about Zen's powers and what they had seen him do.

"For so many years I was a ghost, how did you bring me back to life?" she turned to Zen and asked. "It's weird but that whole time now feels like a time in the fog it's very hard to remember what I felt at all in that form."

Zen then told her he couldn't bring back the dead but since she was turned into a spirit, he was able to put that spirit into a body. He said this was his first time doing anything like this so he really has no idea what she would remember or if she would just be mad about what happened or happy for a new start. "I just figured no matter what, you deserved another chance."

"It's hard for me to think about being mad at my past at this moment. I have been given such a wonderful gift. I know that terrible things happened to me, but I feel young and happy like I did before that."

Zen smiled as he looked at her, "I'm glad" he said.

For the next week, they all walked and enjoyed their time together talking about life and what the future might hold. Zen as always mostly stayed behind just watching and listening, but he was slowly becoming more comfortable with his connection to them even though he wouldn't start a conversation, he was not afraid to answer questions if asked. During that time Cat became more and more like a big brother to Mary and she started to feel very safe with all of them.

They still had about another week of walking left, when one night they had to camp outside as there was no town, or shelter in sight. Zen started a fire and made some extra blankets as it was cold and they were up high. They all settled around the fire and were now eating when they heard a strange sound. At first, they ignored it but then when they heard it repeatedly, Mary got up and sat down next to Cat.

Then a voice out of the dark says "Why has Zendaria come to my mountain, is he here to collect us?"

Zen stood up and walked a few feet toward the voice, "I will not hurt anyone who is not a threat to us."

"I have your word as a Zendarian then?" The voice asked.

"Yes," he replied.

Then slowly out of the dark came a large person cloaked so you could not see their appearance.

Zen said, "You are welcome, we have a fire and some food."

He came close and took off his hood and there stood one of the last remaining Nekomata.

"I am Hideyoshi the Great. If it pleases you, I invite you and your guests to my place."

"We would be honored," Zen said.

They followed him closely as he made his way through a winding pass up the side of the mountain to what appeared to be a cave. But a few feet into the cave was a large heavy door and Hideyoshi opened the heavy door and they all went in. He had transformed the inside of the cave into a beautiful living area, and it even had a fireplace that had a small vent going up and out the rock to camouflage the smoke and not alert someone it was there.

Hideyoshi took off his cloak and he had on Body armor but not the type they had ever seen before.

He loosened the top pieces and laid them on the ground, so he was walking around in just pants. He looked just like a giant white tiger standing on two legs with a body type like a large human and he had long white hair around his face.

He went to the back and brought out a tray that had smoked meat on it. And he sat it on the table and offered it to them. Then went and got what appeared to be wine skins and poured them drinks.

All of them were sitting down at the table and Hideyoshi too made his way to them and took his seat. He saw Mary staring at him but so was everyone else. He was like nothing any of them had ever seen and he was just so magnificent looking and exotic.

Hideyoshi says "I'm sorry am I being immodest, I have not had human company in a long time."

"No, No, it's just that you are so beautiful," said Mary, making him smile. But the smile sort of made him look more menacing.

"So, you're sure you are not here for me?" Hideyoshi asked.

"I wish I was. It would be amazing to watch you fight, but I had no idea you would be here or existed. I'm sorry," said Zen.

"So where are you headed Zendaria" he asked.

"We are headed to the old Elven Castle of Balnictoon, I have been guided there to find an object."

"Well, be careful, the humans around those parts are terrible and not very bright," Hideyoshi said.

"May I ask how long you have been here? Aren't you from the Far East?" asked Zen.

"Yes, I am but I've been here 100s of years now I guess I lost track of time after a while." Stopping what he was doing and looking off in the distance, Hideyoshi said, "I trekked this way about I think three hundred years ago. I was given a vision, I am to wait here for a Zendarian to come and collect me but I'm not sure what that means. I was told that when that happened it would lead to an amazingly glorious death. However, you are now the second Zendaria I have met and now it seems I will continue to wait."

"May I ask why you are called the Great?" asked Duncan.

"Long ago I led the Nekomata army, and we defeated the last major kingdom of the Mermen. It was terrible and lasted for 20 years and left both of our populations at the beginning of a death spiral," he said with a sigh.

"There are less than 10,000 of my kind now, there is no Merman on shores that I know of, but I've heard there still are many in the oceans."

"Am I a Nekomata" asked Cat?

"No, you don't have the features of one my friend," Hideyoshi answered.

"You met the last Zendarian, can you tell me about him," asked Zen.

"His name was Asger, and he was a tall, large man not as big as your friend but mighty nonetheless. He was as hard and fierce as the lands he came from. My race loves to be in the mountains, so I had just started to turn this cave into a place I could live, and he was at my doorway one morning. I asked if he was looking for me, but he wasn't, he just needed a place to rest."

"He by himself had just fought a small Elven war party but they still had 30 or 40 in that group. Those are seriously skilled warriors, and this guy took them out."

"I found what was left of them later. He rested a few days and asked me what I wanted I said a great sturdy door that works and a fireplace that is vented and no one can see the smoke and then I watched him put his hands on the walls and not only did I get that, but he smoothed all these walls for me and the floor to a polished rock."

"That is interesting I was told he was a hard man. Everyone on his quest left him," Zen said.

"Could be true. No one was with him then and he was hard to talk to, but he showed appreciation, which is something, that made living here a dream come true."

They continued for the rest of the night all trading stories deep into the night and the guys told him what they had seen Zen do after which all went to sleep. The next morning before they left Zen asked him what he wanted, and Hideyoshi asked for better health as he was starting to get older for his race so Zen granted it.

As they were leaving Hideyoshi said, "Well if you are ever told to collect me you know I'm here, and let me give you this." It was a medallion with a cat warrior engraved on it. "If you ever run into another of my races show them this and they will show you hospitality otherwise my kind don't want company." It would be three more days before they got to the castle.

As they started walking out of a large forest they found a ruined ancient castle on the side of a large hill with ancient battle scars still all over the landscape and buildings. As they came closer to it a small gang of men came up over the rocks to the right of the ruins. Cat quickly pushed Mary behind him.

Where the hell do you think you're going?" asked the leader of the group.

Zen explained, "We are looking for something that the old Elven King owned, and I would like to trade for it."

"All the elves are dead here, they have been gone for years, you won't find any of them around" proclaimed the men's leader.

Zen then said, "Well it is a small bracelet that looks like green stone but this one has a crescent moon carved in it repeatedly." The Leader said, "Never heard of it. Now get lost!"

Zen then froze time as he had been doing every day as practice, the others just never knew. He went and touched the leader and saw the bracelet he was looking for.

Going back to where he was and unfreezing time Zen said "If you give me that bracelet, I will give you whatever you want."

The leader, getting more annoyed said "Listen we don't have it. Now leave before we make you."

Zen then says "I know your mother wears this bracelet still, your swords are cheap and are not a serious weapon but if you give me the bracelet then I will give you all new swords."

The men were taken aback and gathered and talked amongst themselves in hushed hurried whispers. Then they sent one of the young men out. He comes back a bit later with the bracelet. "Where are the swords?" He asked.

Zen pointed up the hill on a large rock, "They are up there in that bag." The leader looks puzzled thinking how he could have gotten them there. The young man ran up there and yelled down "They are all here," so the leader gave the bracelet over.

Zen turns to his group and says "Don't run but start walking very fast for that tree line these guys are coming after us."

Cat said "Let me at them,"

"Cat, you will have your time but for now protect Mary and take her to the wood line."

57

They start hearing the men yell and call out to the group and in gross ways to Mary. When Zen hears that he stops dead and turns around. "I will not have this talk," Zen exclaims and the group of men laugh as they are running toward him. The rest of Zen's group watched from the tree line.

Zen then says, "If you take one more step your deaths are on you. This is my last warning." The men do stop for a moment then look at each other, start laughing, and start moving toward him.

Zen started saying something something the group couldn't make out and 10 trees behind the group began to float up 30 feet into the air and shatter into a million pieces. Zen is now moving his arm in small and then larger circles stopping with his arm thrust out and the shattered pieces fly with great velocity into all the men. Most die instantly but the leader is lying in extreme pain bleeding out. Zen said "This is on you, your families will suffer now having no men in the village to look after them," clenching his fist in front of the man all the swords turned into dust and Zen walked away.

As he walked toward the group, they didn't know what to say. They are happy he took care of the problem yet at the same time scared at what he did. He stood in front of them and said "I gave them a fair warning. I told them the deaths would be on them."

Duncan said "We understand why you did it, but you must admit the way you did it was so supernatural it just scared us a little. We are still with you just you don't see that every day."

Zen let out a sigh. "I'm sorry. I can understand that is a lot to take in." Deep down inside Zen feared that they would start acting like his neighbors and others did fearing him like in the past. He was told that the last Zendaria scared all his companions, and they all left him fearful.

"Well let's get moving," said Mary, changing the subject. "I need to go see the ocean."

Chapter 9

At the end of traveling on the second day, Mary was standing alone watching the children from the local village play. Zen slowly walked up behind her and said nothing but watched the children laughing and having a good time. Mary said without turning around, "They reminded her of her and her siblings playing when they were young."

"I'm sure you must really miss them," Zen responds.

"They seem like just a dream now; it was so long ago," she responded.

"Can I ask you a question, do you know if I can have children? I mean maybe since you made this body maybe it can't," she asked.

"To be honest I don't know but I would think so," Zen responds. "I mean all the parts should be working," Zen said with a smile.

"Would you like to have children?" Zen asked.

"With the right man," looking sideways at Zen, "Yes! Ever since I was very little, I thought I would like to be a mom," Mary said.

"There is nothing more beautiful and more important in this world than a good mom," Zen smiled and said. "I hope you get to then, Mary, you deserve to be happy," Zen says.

"Have you ever wanted them? Children, I mean," Mary asked.

"I never really thought about it, I guess it would be nice, but I don't know what my future might hold. I never knew my father.

He died before I was born. I think it is better when the father is around."

"Have you ever wanted to be married?" Mary asked.

"Yes of course but I'm sure anyone would be interested in someone who might be so different from them and may not be here very long. I think they probably want someone more like them, someone they can grow old with," Zen says.

"What do you mean?" asked Mary.

"Well at the end of this quest, I must go to my final test, and if I'm not strong or wise enough I will die."

"You can die?" She blurted out.

"Of course," he responded.

"I don't want you to die," she said quietly.

"Me neither," he giggled.

"How can I help you pass?" Mary asked, with her brows furrowed and sheer determination on her face.

"I really have no idea but thinking of you, having a good life, and being happy makes me happy, so you help me there already," Zen explains.

There was so much more that she wanted to say but couldn't find the words, so she just stayed silent and studied her toes after she had taken her saddle off and was gripping the dirt with them.

After a long pause and watching the children, Zen starts to walk away but stops and turns to Mary.

"I know your life may not have worked out the way you would have liked, but you are the coolest woman I have ever run into." Both of their eyes locked for a moment, but Zen turned away feeling the power in her eyes, and walked away. He headed to the rest of the group at the inn where they had gotten rooms for the night.

They had been traveling for a few days when one day Zen stopped suddenly. He had been quite ahead of the group and as they caught up to him, he took off his hood, looked to his left, and stared into the distance for quite a while.

"We need to go this way for a few hours. There is a house we need to go see," he told the group as they caught up to him.

Duncan said, "We will follow you anywhere but is there a reason we must go that way suddenly?"

Zen softly says "The wind is whispering to me, there is someone extraordinary down this way." After a few hours, they found a large, exquisite stone building surrounded by ornate gardens on the side of a large hill. Zen walks up to the large wooden front door and just before he knocks, it opens, revealing a man.

"I was not sure you would come. Come in, my honored guests."

He was a very slim tall man who looked like the people hieroglyphs craved into the stone built across the ocean in the desert kingdoms. His tan skin was smooth and perfect and somehow made him seem royal. He took the group into a large room and sat them all at a table. He called for his servant Gregnow to serve tea and pie, then excused himself and headed out of the room.

The servant was a very short man who had sharp features and was dressed immaculately. He took care of all our needs as the first man came back into the room and sat at the head of the table. "My name is Akhenaten, I am honored to have you as guests." The group all said, "Thank you!"

Duncan then turned to Zen and said "Is he the guy who was whispering to you?" Zen looked sort of embarrassed "Yes, he is."

Akhenaten then said, "Your master is indeed powerful I could feel him walk by and I was hoping he would hear me." Zen then spoke up "I'm not their master, we are all just friends."

Akhenaten had no idea what to make of him saying that. "Strange customs I guess. But nonetheless, you are powerful. May I ask how old you are?"

Zen said "I'm 19." The entire group looked in shock as they all assumed he was much older by the way he acted, and he had never said his age out loud before. "No that is impossible please don't lie to me boy," demanded Akhenaten.

Zen corrected himself, "I am almost 19 earth years old, but I have over 1200 years of human experiences collected lifetimes in me." "Ah that is what I sense," said Akhenaten. "How is that possible?"

Zen then went on to explain his story from the start-up to that moment with Duncan and Cat, piping in with different details or connecting stories. "So you are the new Zendaria, it is an honor to meet you. I have known a few over the years," said Akhenaten.

Zen then said, "There is only one every few centuries."

"Yes, I am almost three thousand years old".

Everyone sat there in shock, no one said anything for a moment. Then Mary asked if he was a human

Since the beginning of man, there is also what is known as a watcher someone who tries his best to keep track of real human history," Said Akhenatan. He then spoke of the last Zandaria and how he was a brutal exacting man who was the strongest human Akhenaten had ever seen in all his years. "However, after traveling the earth he disappeared, and I have not heard of anyone till you Zen."

Zen then went on to tell him that after a Quest there was a final test, and he was destroyed. Mary whipped her head around and asked, "When is this test?"

"We are on my quest now so when it reaches its end, I will be tested and hopefully I will survive," says Zen.

"How does one pass?" asked Akhenaten

"I don't know, I'm just supposed to make myself as strong as possible and try to make myself as ready as I can. Whatever that means," explained Zen.

"I hope you do," Akhenaten says.

After dining Akhenaten invited Zen to his rooftop terrace and Gregnow showed the rest to the large room they will be staying in. The room had a sheet in one corner, making a makeshift wall to cut off a section for Mary's privacy. "What do you suppose they are talking about?" Mary pondered. "Cool stuff I'm sure," replied Duncan feeling left out.

Gregnow in a very slow deep voice then spoke for the first time and said, "If you need anything no matter what the time ring that bell and I will come. Good night," and closed the door behind him.

"What a fancy place this is," admired Mary, the stonework on the walls featured intricate carvings, beautiful long rugs, and paintings hung on the walls. There was a large fireplace, which was empty now, and the furniture not just in the room but the whole place was like that of a king.

Meanwhile, up on the roof terrace, Akhenaten went on to tell Zen he was first from the ancient desert kingdoms to the south and how below them was a vast Forrest full of lakes, rivers, and all sorts of creatures more than a man could comprehend. Zen asked, "How come you are here now?"

Akhenaten then walked over to the side of the roof and pointed down to a large garden in the back of the house. In the middle at the top of it was a grave and a statue of a woman. Zen said, "Oh I see how long has she been gone?"

"Almost 50 yrs., I just cannot leave her. I built this place for her". Akhenaten said staring out into the garden.

"Living so long must be hard to lose your loved ones and continue," Zen asks.

"HA" laughed Akhenaten, "no one who lives long thinks that. Most of those thoughts come from mortals with no imagination. Don't get me wrong losing them hurts and it takes years to overcome the great ones, but time does heal all wounds. Remember that. After a while, you see that no one will match your love for that one person but that in a while something different comes and it is beautiful in its own way. It can be enjoyed just as much although differently. It is in the variety that comes the real beauty."

"Look around and see all the variety of each plant, tree, landscape, people and species for God loves variety, and everything is beautiful in its own way. Most creatures never take the time to notice."

Zen thinking said, "That makes sense, I'll have to think about that."

"But here is the weird part is that as different as we can be we are also equally the same. Same flower just a different color and it might look vastly different when in fact, it is not really that different. After you lived a long time or have all that experience that you have, you can understand people. Yes, each one reacts a little differently, but humans are usually consistent and over time you can see and know what will happen before it does. Inexperienced ones think you can see the future but really you have just seen how most humans react in different situations before and can expect repetition," Akhenaten said.

"I think the difference between us is you experienced it for yourself, and I experienced it through someone else which makes me struggle with who I am, what would I do. If that makes sense," Zen replied.

"Well, I would think it's not much different, I just watched and learned how they react over time and you just did it faster and know why they did what they did. They can't hide anything from you. I think you will see the similarities in time. And you don't have to question yourself. But that is also part of being young and sometimes old," Akhenaten said with a laugh.

At that moment, Gregnow brought up drinks for the two men as both discussed life and its meaning.

After some time, Akhenaten looked up from his drink, "You are much different than any Zendaria I've met! And I have run into, I would say, about a half dozen throughout history. Some are strong and some are kind but you, you are humble, which is almost nonexistent for a god."

Zen said softly "I don't see myself as a god, I'm just trying to find people and help them. Making friends with some along the way has been a great gift to me but it's a two-way street we both get something out of it."

"That is just it, I don't think any of your kind ever thought that. I think they saw them as tools, but I don't think they knew the meaning of the word friend," said Akhenaten.

"To me, that seems like a sad existence," Zen said drinking from his cup.

"Zen I truly do enjoy this conversation and meeting you, but I need some help" Akhenaten explained.

Zen remarked, "I figured something was coming."

"I am at the end of my time; I have been waiting for the next watcher to be born but I have not found them yet and I worry that maybe I'm the last of my kind. Either way, I don't want to die in the dust but rather in my bed."

"There is a man coming named Vannick and he has a small gang of mercenaries with him. He wants my head as a trophy for his master, he knows I'm a watcher and he wants to take this place and the secret vault of treasures underneath. If you would stop him for me, I will give you this place after I die and everything in the vault below. However, as a show of good faith, I will give you now my most prized possession, the ancient breastplate of the High priest to the true God. There are not many other things so sacred on earth. But for you, I will add one more gift, I will allow you to touch me and get all my experiences." Says Akhenaten.

Zen, thought about the offer a bit before accepting. "When do you expect him?" he asked.

Akhenaten didn't know but knew it would not be long. "You can all stay with me and take advantage of my hospitality till then," he added with a little laugh.

"My men and I will start keeping watch at night," Zen said.

Akhenaten stopped him and said, "Sneaking in at night is not Vannick's style. He will come in the day so everyone around would know him."

After talking for many hours Zen went down to get some sleep, when he came into the room, he had three very anxious people pretending they were not waiting for him to hear what happened. Zen explained what they talked about and what they would have to do. He asked Cat to especially be on guard to protect everyone but maybe the size of you will scare them off.

That night Mary dreamed that Zen and her lived in Akhenaten's house and had many children, but her dream turned, and she was all alone again because Zen didn't want to be with someone with her past and all that had happened to her. When he said those words in her dream it hurt her so much it woke her up from a dead sleep. She then lay there still for many hours.

After a few days, they heard a horn in the distance blowing. "That will be Vannick," Gregnow proclaimed. "Be careful. He has powers as well but nothing like your power Zen."

Zen tells Mary and Duncan to stay with Akhenaten, takes Cat, and walks out the side entrance of the house down the dust-covered stone road built centuries ago. They saw Vannick on horseback with 6 other men of various sizes slowly come up to the two and Vannick jumps off his horse. "I have no idea what that Demon has told you, but he must die, and we are not going be stopped by some good Samaritans no matter how large they are."

"Just go back to where you came from. I don't want to hurt you. I am the old man's protector." Zen told Vannick.

Vannick laughed and shouted, "So the old man bought some mercenaries. Well, you know boy dying is no way to make a living." Vannick pulls out his sword and somehow makes a magic shield on his forearm and starts running toward them. At the same time the men in the back start getting off their horses and start doing the same. Cat who has no weapons roars like a lion and pulls Zen behind him.

Zen stops time and thinks, 'If I kill these guys, I might scare my guys again like the forest fight. How can I scare this guy, so he gets the point and leaves the old man alone but doesn't kill him.' With everyone frozen, he went and sat on a nearby rock to think. He realizes it might be nice if Cat did have some sort of weapon to defend himself, but he has no idea how to use it, what about a time maybe when I'm not around? Then Zen goes back to his place and unfreezes time. With that, an air blast knocks Vannick back into his men. Then the air around them starts to swirl faster and faster

69

till a tornado opens above and around them. But the men are right directly in the eye of the storm, so they are just lying in a pile watching with horror.

As the Tornado gains speed and size, a calm Zen walks toward the tornado. Cat yells out to Zen, "Get out of there."

But Zen, completely unaffected, walked into the storm and straight through untouched. Not even one hair on his full head of brown hair moved in the wind. As he appeared on the other side to the men inside. He used the tornado to somehow amplify his voice so not just those in the storm but even outside could hear him proclaim "Vannick, you and your man have been found lacking. Take this as a warning from Zen, the master of the elements, if you come here again you will not leave alive." And Zen then walked back out of the storm and the storm moved and picked up the men and the horses and shot them into the lake about a half mile away. Zen however made sure the water took all of them in and didn't kill any of them.

Cat screamed with delight with his arm in the air, "That was amazing Zen!"

Together, the two walked back to the rest of the group watching from the roof of Akhenaten's home. All of them were cheering, even Akhenaten and Gregnow joined in, not believing what they just watched. As they came down to meet the two and congratulate them Zen just smiled and said, "I didn't kill them." looking sheepishly at Mary. "Hey I came up with that name, Master of Elements," proclaimed Duncan proudly. "If it becomes popular, I want credit," he added laughingly. But he was so proud

Zen had used the name he had jokingly come up with on the boat at the start of their journey.

They all surrounded him and walked into the house. Gregnow prepared a special feast, and everyone enjoyed themselves and lived in the moment of the victory not thinking what might be waiting in the future.

That night when Zen laid his head down, the Guide came to him, "That was an interesting way to handle that situation," it said. "I was trying to show my friends I'm not a scary monster but that I believe in the sanctity of life," Zen explained. "A worthy endeavor I'm sure," the Guide said, "and the gifts the Watcher has given you or will give are more than anyone could ask for."

Zen said, "Yes, I won't hold him to those if he doesn't want to."

The Guide then said "If he fulfills these gifts tell him that I will make sure the new watcher comes to see him before he dies as a gift to him. She was born and is already a couple of hundred years old but lives in the very far east and has yet to make her way here."

As Zen woke that morning and after breakfast, he met Akhenaten on the roof, and he handed him a gold breast adorned with fine gems on the front. "This is the holiest thing I have ever owned; I hope it brings you good fortune and provides protection for you on your journey," he said. "Now for your other gift.. come," said Akhenaten and reached out his hand, which Zen then took. However almost three thousand years of experience was more than he ever received at once, and Zen passed out.

While he was out, he saw many things and watched Akhenaten with his many lovers over the years and the deeper moments of his relationships, trials, and triumphs. Saw Him rise to great power for a while but then disappear and live a quieter life only to rise again someplace different later. He watched as his love grew for his last wife Alicja. Watched them fight and love and her grow old but he cared for her till the end and even still.

That made him then start to dream about Mary but in his dream, she was very sad, and Zen couldn't figure out why. Mary told him that he forced her to stay with him and she wasted her second chance feeling she had to repay him by staying with him after what he did. With that thought, Zen finally woke up only to find himself in his bed, with Mary sitting by his side.

"Everyone, he is waking up," she yelled.

"How long was I out?" asks Zen

"Three days," Mary told him.

"How do you feel?" she asked.

"I really need something to drink," asked Zen.

With everyone now around his bed, Akhenaten apologized and hoped that he was alright.

"It was a lot to take in, I was living all those years, my body and brain taking in the emotions and skills and experiences. Akhenaten you have lived a fantastic life, you are truly a good man," said Zen.

Akhenaten smiled but said nothing back.

"What do you need now?" asked Duncan, "If you can bring me some food and water, that would be good and I need more time to take in this gift," Zen replied.

Since the day of the attack, Cat has been walking around seeing if anyone was coming or if Vannick didn't get the hint but no one came and everyone in the area was only talking about the man who can control the elements. After about a week, Zen came out of the room he was in and said he was good to go. Akhenaten told him in front of Gregnow that after he dies the house will belong to Zen and if he is not around, he could leave it to who he wants it to go to. Gregnow would live and take care of it till then. After Akhenaten told them all what his final wishes were, Zen told him that the Guide had come to him, and his gift was that the new Watcher would come and spend time with him before he died. Zen tells the three of them to get ready and they will start back out south to that ocean city they were going to before this stop.

That night Guide came back to Zen, "You will go and meet a man at an Inn in the town of Cnossus which is before the Ocean city of Eretria. 10 days from now when the sun is at its highest, he will come in. But be careful, this one might not join your group, or he might want to leave the group after a while. So allow him to make the choice." He then went on to tell Zen the importance of the next few weeks.

Chapter 10

In the whole City of Eretria, there is no place more opulent, more revered than the High Wizards palace. It has ancient treasures and statues filling its courtyards and its now 200-year existence reigns the most powerful High Wizard of them all, High Wizard Amedeo. He was throwing his yearly bash that would bring all the mages and wizards in the area and some from great distances to come and compare notes and ideas for the future and contend for position and power.

A hooded man walked up to the blacksmith and asked, "Where is the High Wizards Palace?" The blacksmith looked up from his work, "Are you kidding? It's the largest building and sits on a hill overlooking the ocean, you can't possibly miss it." However, he was just using the question as an excuse to see who was living there with the Blacksmith and there stood a young girl with very bright red hair. "Well now aren't you a cutie, tell me what your name is little girl?" "Clio," she responded to which he smiled, then thanked the blacksmith and went to the palace.

This year brought all sorts of types of people in, and the city was more packed than usual. As this time of year brought merchants and others, as they know the festivities bring more opportunities from all over.

However, this year also came this hooded stranger to these parts and his sheer presence made others uncomfortable. It would feel as if death was near or a cold chill and made one feel an emptiness inside. As he made his way through the crowd, he tried not to bring too much attention to himself. But with so many people with magic present, and the feeling his mere presence would give them, he couldn't stay in one place too long so they couldn't figure out it was him. In this era by the way he was dressed, he could be taken for an assassin and his coat and hood concealed him so you didn't know what he might be carrying.

When he got to the palace, he found a way in and stayed on the move as he walked around it and sized the place up. He needed to get to the high wizard, but he was not sure what might be the safest way to do that. Surely now waiting in a line but soon he needed to duck out as everyone started to become afraid.

As High Wizard Amedeo gathered his guests in the grand courtyard and told them about this year's festivities The stranger slowly moved around the courtyard to the back private garden that few ever saw and was the private place for Amedeo to think and ponder problems.

After that, the High Wizard invited all his guests into the feasting hall where they would all dine and enjoy his entertainment. Just then one of his advisors noticed the figure in his private garden. "Sir you can't be here." The hooded man stood up and said, "I need a private audience with the High Wizard." He then made the Advisor turn cold and feel empty inside and hurt. Scared, the advisor said, "Give me a moment." He turned and left to get the High Wizard and the man sat back down.

Shortly the High Wizard showed up with the advisor and 2 guards, "What is the meaning of this disrespect?" demanded Amedeo.

The hooded man stood up and took his hood off, there stood a handsome brash man with dark features in his early 30s. "My name is Brewst and I have come a long way to find someone and to help you."

"If you didn't notice, we are in the middle of the yearly feast, surely you should know your place and wait till the reception," Amedeo said sternly.

"I can't do that Your Honor; my presence will only scare your guests if I stay too long. That fear will become panic and that only leads to bad things. If you give me just a few moments I will explain, and you can go back to your dinner, and I will wait here for you." Brewst Explains

"Enough of this," said Amedeo angrily, and turned to walk away. "Tell me High wizard do you feel fear when you see me? Do your insides fill with dread? I can explain that to you," says Brewst.

Amedeo stops and looks at the others "I'll be okay. Leave us for a moment." He turns and sits down across from Brewst. "Yes, I do feel strange around you. Why is it? Are you evil?"

"I have no power at all, I am something completely different. You see I can see people's power or magic. It is not just something you pull from the air or ground, it is like a being that lives within you and you two share a common goal, to stay alive," Brewst explains.

"This is nonsense there is no such thing. I am the most learned Wizard on this side of the world and I have never read or heard about this. You're wasting my time." As Amedeo stood up to leave, Brewst said, "I will prove it to you."

"How?" demanded Amedeo.

"I can take away someone's power. I'll only do this to show you so when you feel it, know I will give it back unharmed. It's just a demonstration."

"You're a fool and a liar," said Amadeo scornfully.

With that Brewst made a small hand gesture and Amedeo's magic was gone. Amedeo felt it immediately and stared at Brewst completely shocked. He started to panic like someone drowning but Brewst grabbed him and helped him calm down. "You see the reason people with magic feel dread when I am around is that their magic or power is afraid. It knows I can take it and so it's trying to communicate with you. It is trying to make you run away from me so you both are safe," Brewst said. "Truly what do you feel?"

Amedeo said, "Sadly I feel empty like when I did when my parents died when I was young, it's an overwhelming sadness." "Ok ok, I will give your power back, now." This time he made a different hand gesture and Amedeo felt it come back over him like waves of comfort, pleasure even. Amedeo fell to his seat with no words.

"Listen High Wizard, go back to your feast but then come here and we will talk about what could be an arrangement to benefit both of us." Amedeo shook his head in agreement and staggered off back to his dinner. After a few hours, a very distracted Amedeo walked back out to Brewst, and as he walked in. Brewst said, "I'm not here as an enemy and can be helpful."

Amedeo still in disbelief, "How is it that I have never heard of a being like you?"

"As far as I know I'm the only one of my kind, I've never met another so maybe we are just rare."

"What has made you come to me?" asks Amedeo

"First let me tell you how I can help you, First I see the magic in all your guests, I can tell you who is powerful and who is faking it. You see I see the magic or power, it's like an aura around each of you. Think of it as a person that lives inside you. I can tell if you're using your magic for evil purposes as it leaves a mark or scar on it or if it's evil also it has a particular smell or color. But your magic can also come to love you and revere you if you work with it in doing good."

Amedeo asks "When you take power what happens?"

"Well, I can do three things with it. One is, I give it back after I prove a point. Two, I can take it and hold it rendering those people powerless, but just for a short time, or three, I can kill or destroy it for lack of a better word. You see it's bound to me, but it also can't attach to me, so it withers and dies. That person then will never have any magic or power ever again," explains Brewst.

"I will tell you the three men you have as your advisors are very weak, they barely do more than tricks," says Brewst. "So, you're saying get rid of them?" asks Amedeo.

"No, they might give great advice and or be great friends always looking out for you, I have no idea. I can just tell you if it came to some sort of battle, they are worthless."

"Also, your special Mage prodigy Yves, is using his magic to sexually assault your young servant girls. His magic though is not evil, so it has many scars and hates him. If you don't believe me, call the youngest girl, you have serving who has been cleaning the rooms here. He comes into the room when she is working, locks the door, molests her, and is cutting around her nipples and below when he sodomizes her," said Brewst.

"Guard, please go and get Neith and tell her I need to see her immediately," ordered Amedeo.

"Do you want me to leave for this?" asks Brewst. "No, you will stay and if you're wrong I will have you killed as Yves is like a son to me." "So be it," remarks Brewst so they sat in silence till the girl came in.

"I have something I need to ask, and it will not be easy," said Amedeo.

"Anything for the high wizard I'm here to serve," says Neith.

"Is Yves hurting you?" asked Amedeo.

The girl says nothing and looks down, her eyes pooling up with tears.

"I will ask you again if Yves hurting you?" demanded Amedeo.

"If I have done something to offend you, sir, I apologize."

Amedeo then demanded she take her top off.

Again, the girl looked down saying, "If I have done something to offend you, sir, I apologize."

Amedeo then says "If you do not lower your top, you will be fired immediately and sent outside the city."

The young girl burst into tears, "Please do not shame me like this, I am the only provider for my ailing mother and father and siblings."

Amedeo gaining his composure says "I'm sorry child, I didn't mean to be harsh. This man here says that Yves is hurting you and cutting your breast and down below. If this is true, you have done nothing wrong, but he will have to be punished for it. I promise if you will put up with this indignity, I will never dishonor you again and will make sure you have a higher station."

The young girl slowly pulls her blouse down and under her breasts, Just as Brewst said, she had many cuts circling her nipples on both breasts. She then spoke quietly, "He told me if I told anyone, he would kill me, and no one here would care since he is your personal prodigy."

Amedeo rage turned into despair and then said, "It is ok girl we do care. Pull your top back up." He then told the Guard to take her to her room and make sure she had plenty to eat and drink and send extra money to her family from me personally thanking them for her service.

"That is heartbreaking, I will have to have him killed, Said Amedeo. "Oh, Yves what have you become?" he added softly.

"I have a better punishment for the boy," Said Brewst. "Let me take his power and then after asking him to do tasks in front of everyone, banish him from the city when proves unable to. He will never have power again and be humiliated. But maybe he can learn his lesson."

"You are a very wise man Brewst, I am sorry I was hostile toward you. I must admit I'm really trying to fight an overwhelming fear inside me."

"Tell me who are the most powerful people here in the city," asks Amedeo.

"Well of course you are by far the most powerful, but you could be more powerful. Second is Artyom."

Amedeo says "Oh he is so abrasive…also what do you mean I could be more powerful?"

"That is how we can both benefit, I will get to that in a minute. After him, Lady Caihong is very powerful but not as much as you two. Third is your stable boy Aeolus, he is completely untrained and has a power stronger than the other two if trained. Then there is the blacksmith's young fiery redheaded daughter, she has the potential to be even stronger than you when she is older if trained properly," explained Brewst.

"You say I'm the most powerful, are there any that are more powerful than me" Asks Amedeo

"You are the fifth most powerful person I know of," tells Brewst. "Who are they?" Amedeo asks

"There is someone so powerful I can feel him from here, I have felt him for the past 10 years. I am trying to find him. He is from a kingdom way up north, but he is on the move, and I think headed this way."

"You say you can feel his power from here, how far away come you feel mine?" asks Amedeo.

"At the city gates I could feel you," adds Brewst. "How powerful must he be, I would love to meet this person," says Amedeo.

"Who are the others you mentioned," asks Amedeo

"Do you remember the High Priest Asher, his magic is still strong as ever," says Brewst.

"But he has been dead for 80 years," says Amedeo puzzled.

"Yes, but his magic loved him totally and holds his body in reverence, in cases like that it's like a loved one, it takes a long time for the magic to leave but it will eventually," added Brewst.

"Does my magic love me Brewst?" asked Amedeo.

"Yes, High Wizard it thinks you are a fair man," said Brewst.

"Then the next is Duke Moritz but his power is Evil, and both have many dark designs so you must be careful around him. Then, The High Wizard Maximilian to the east is a little more powerful than you," says Brewst.

Amedeo sat in awe of all that he was hearing, "How may I get more powerful Brewst?" he asked.

"The most powerful, he has many abilities but one of them is to change or heal flesh, he has many abilities, but he could fix your physical affliction," Brewst says.

"How do you know?" asks an embarrassed Amedeo.

"Your power tells it all but if you made your body whole your power could go to another level not to mention the ability to pleasure someone," Says Brewst.

"What do we need to do," asked Amedeo

"Well, that is how we can both help each other. I want to meet this person, but I am no one, There is no reason for him to give me the time of day. But if I could go to him as your advisor and invite him here, we both could get what we want," plans Brewst.

"OK that's a deal but before you go, please remove Yves' power and I will upgrade Aeolus to my new prodigy and invite the daughter to come and be trained here in the palace," Amedeo says.

"I will have the innovation drawn up by the house master and you can leave tomorrow to find him but now let me give you lodging for the night and some food," said Amedeo. So, the two went back to the hall where everyone had been feasting a few hours ago, but only a few were left now. Amedeo and Brewst talked through the night and Amedeo told Brewst that he was from a long line of Wizards and that a few in his family line had been High Wizards. He grew up in a small town in the southern part of the kingdom of Italy. Because of his affliction, Amedeo had never been with someone but he would love nothing more than to find love.

Brewst said that when he was about seven, his parents died of an illness within months of each other which put him and his older sister on the streets trying to make it in the world as best as they could. His sister married a nice older man who took good care of her. Brewst stayed with them for a few years and the older man made sure he got some education but as soon as he could he hit the road, he did and has been traveling ever since.

He had been all over Europe and to the east seeing parts of Asia and even the southern dessert kingdoms on the other side of the great sea. He loved being on the move and making his way and since he was naturally very smart, his skills only made it easy to get his way. He was a great storyteller and loved collecting experiences, and people's stories and sharing them. Spoke in a way that made people comfortable with him unless they had power inside them but even then, he could sometimes overcome it. He liked to think of himself as a man of the world and dangerous, but he was just very charming and great at reading people.

Chapter 11

After walking to the first city Zen mentioned, they stayed at an inn for a few days, and all of them. While staying there each one found different ways of occupying themselves wandering around, Mary could not help but watch the young children playing in the square. Duncan usually would look for a brothel and Cat would always stay in Mary's vicinity to make sure she was protected as Zen had instructed him. Mary would come to look at him like a big brother, and she loved teasing him.

He wanted to be her protector, but he wanted to protect them all. He was so thankful for this family he had found and the gifts he had been given he would do anything to protect that.

After a few hours, Duncan comes back to the inn and turns to Zen, "I know it is not really my place but why are we just sitting here?" he asks.

"I'm going to be meeting someone downstairs in a short while," said Zen.

"Will they be joining us?" asked Duncan.

"I don't know yet, we will have to see what he chooses," said Zen.

After that, both Zen and Duncan go downstairs and order drinks and wait, when a hooded man walks up to him and says, "Sir you have been invited to the palace of the High Wizard" and hands over the invitation. As Zen takes the envelope, he touches the man's hand.

"Why do you approach me under false pretense?" asks Zen.

The hooded man was shocked and stood silent for a moment. He knew how powerful this man was, and he was hoping not to start off by displeasing him. He thought about making up a story or maybe running but he figured he better come clean and hope for mercy.

Then he removed his hood and sat down with them. "My name is Brewst, I am a traveler from the West and have been looking for you for a long time. I didn't think you would just meet with a nobody, so I talked the High Wizard into inviting you to his palace," explains Brewst.

"What kind of a name is Brewst?" says Duncan.

"A great one!" barks back Brewst.

"Well that surely takes ingenuity to pull that off but you're more than a traveler aren't you?" pressed Zen.

"Can you read my mind? How do you know everything?" Brewst said puzzled.

Brewst was wondering, even before the meeting, can he feel me like the others. Is his power scared of me? Could I take it?

Zen says, "You are dying to find out, why don't you try?"

"Wow that was fast," said Brewst. "I didn't see it going this way. But," with a gleam in his eyes, he added, "Why not?"

In the next few seconds, Brewst wakes up lying on the floor. "Where are we," he asks

"We are in a void; I can not only stop time but open a pocket in the spiritual plane and ponder things," explains Zen.

"So, it didn't work," Brewst says as he is picking himself up off the floor. "No, it didn't. But you are strong enough that my power protected itself and pulled us both here." Brewst then started to explain himself, but Zen stopped him, "I already know everything. Once I touch your skin all your experiences and skills transfer to me."

"You mean I have lost everything?" a dejected Brewst asked.

"No, you are unharmed. I just now know every moment of your life. I find it interesting your power and that you have known about me for years is amazing, shows how powerful you are."

"I guess I never thought of it that way before. Will I remember anything after we leave here?" he asked.

"I will allow you to remember everything, I was sent here you know to meet you," said Zen, and then proceeded to tell him the story from the beginning to this moment.

"So, you stop time, I can't wrap my head around that. So, when you do you can move but you can't move others," asks Brewst.

"Correct," said Zen.

"How does this void work, where are we again?" asked Brewst.

"Where we exactly are I have no idea, I would guess we are right at that bar but in a pocket on the spiritual side instead of the physical. Remember there is no such thing as time to them, it is just a human construct," explains Zen.

Zen then went on to explain what he and the others were doing and how they all came together.

"Really, she was an evil spirit that is crazy!" exclaimed Brewst. "I think she would prefer a haunting spirit," added Zen.

Brewst then asks "So, let me ask you, you have all the memories and feelings, so you know what it's like giving and taking in a sexual relationship is that weird? And when you screw someone, you're touching them so is it like you're screwing yourself, whoa that is heavy man I must think about that for a bit. You kinky devil you!"

Zen just smiled and said, "I like you, let's head back and meet the others." and in a moment, they were back in the bar. Brewst immediately sits down and puts his hand out, "I'm sorry Duncan let me properly introduce myself." Duncan immediately turned to Zen, "You did the thing huh?"

"Yea it was crazy," exclaimed Brewst.

"Well let's go meet the others," Duncan says.

After introducing him to the rest of the group they went and ate dinner and Brewst asked them all a million questions. Brewst comes across as a very confident cocky type of man, who dresses like an assassin or a pirate just because he thinks it looks cool and tough. Yet he is not a jerk and has a soft side. He knows women and men alike are attracted to him because how can't they be he thinks? He is the life of every party and he fits right in with their mostly shy group, besides Duncan. He also has an uncanny ability to read people and the situation.

As it was getting late and they started heading to their rooms to sleep, Duncan turned to Brewst and said "So what do you think? Will you join us?"

Brewst had a blank expression on his face.

"He didn't tell you; he was sitting here waiting for you because you're supposed to join us on our journey," says Duncan.

Brewst looked at Zen who said, "If you are here at daybreak, we know you are with us, and we will go meet your friend the High Wizard."

As Brewst walked out of the inn and to the place he was staying, for the first time he felt like he belonged, like there was nothing else on earth he would rather be doing than hanging out with Zen and his group. He had never felt that way before.

At Daybreak, the group came out and saw Brewst sitting on the stool in front of the inn. "Wow you're here early," said Cat.

"To be honest I went and got my stuff and sat here all night so I would not miss you all," Brewst responded.

As the day continued the group kept talking and Zen trailed just a few paces behind just listening and taking it all in. Over the course of a few days and nights, that they spent camping, Brewst spent time with each one and collectively as a group to get to know everyone better. Each night after Zen helped get something to eat for everyone each one took a turn telling their own story and then they all would bring up parts of the story that they now all shared, each explaining what Zen had done and how much it meant to them. It was still hard for Zen to feel like he could share his feelings the same way but taking care of his friends made him feel good and helped him understand who he really was. Brewst noticed this time that when Mary talked about Zen the look in her eyes said more than her words, but he just listened.

Brewst caught up to Mary on the walk the next day and said, "I could see how the rest of us fit in and what we bring to the party but besides being smoking hot what power do you have?"

He wasn't trying to provoke her but to see if she would say more about what her eyes said last night.

"I have no powers at all, I can't really do anything special, I guess I'm along for.." she stopped mid-sentence and paused for a long moment. "…the ride," she finished.

"Whoa I'm sorry I didn't see it," says Brewst.

"See what," asked Mary.

"You love him," Brewst says.

She just looked flustered and tried to start a few different sentences but nothing really came out. "Have you told him?" asked Brewst.

She accepted the situation and gave in and just shook her head no. "How could he love someone like me? I was a floating screaming head when we first met," sort of laughing.

"First impressions," giggled Brewst.

"He watched all the terrible things they did to me before they killed me. He deserves someone pure. Someone with a heart not full of pain and hate," explains Mary.

"None of that was your fault and I have only been here for a minute, but I don't think he thinks like that at all. You should tell him. Not to mention that he gave you a second chance and you're not some 300-year-old lady, you're a freshly minted 18. He could not have given you more. If we were all on some sort of quest to his final test, and he does die, I think you are going to regret not telling him more than anything, and that says a lot with you," says Brewst.

"I wish it was that easy but all of us being together it's hard to express how I feel. Plus, he is so intimidating and quiet that I'm not sure what he is thinking. I would hate to bring it up and if he just didn't feel that way, it would just be awkward for me to be here with you all. I have nowhere else to go so I don't want to ruin my chance to be here and be part of this / His family."

"I understand Mary, I do. I just think it is a mistake not to take that chance. I guess the question is, is love worth the chance? That it could go all wrong, or will it be worth never knowing what you could have had."

Mary said nothing more just kept walking as the tears streamed down her cheeks so Brewst gave her space and fell back to Zen. However, for a long time, neither said anything just walked in silence.

"Why didn't you tell me a spirit told you to meet me and add me to your journey?" Brewst asked Zen.

"Well because it also said that there is a chance you will betray us or leave us, so I figured it best to just see how things play out."

"Ouch man that really hurts," Brewst interjected.

"Don't take it personally, you might leave us for something good, but it must be your choice. Talking to the spirit that is big on God's list is freedom of choice," says Zen.

"Did they say that with the others?" asked Brewst.

"No but maybe it was because of how we ended up together, and you are a free spirit so you must decide differently," said Zen.

"Zen, can I ask, I can see how useful the guys are but why is Mary here with us?" asked Brewst slyly trying to get a reaction out of him.

Zen for a long moment didn't say anything then turned to Brewst. However, Brewst didn't allow Zen to say anything. "You love her, don't you?" Brewst asked.

Zen didn't say anything, just smirked.

"Why don't you tell her? I think she would respond positively," said Brewst.

"Look what I have given her, she could just be feeling that she owes me or maybe due to my power it is putting her in a spot where she feels that what she is supposed to do instead of what she, deep down, in her heart wants," explains Zen.

"Why not just touch her to find out?" demanded Brewst.

"Again, it would be my power making the decision, not her," Zen says softly.

"I would rather her show that to me somehow first before I put her in the spot," Zen says.

"So, we are walking to your death, and you don't want to find out if you found the love you say you are looking for this whole time before you go. I guarantee you are going regret it in those final moments my man," scolded Brewst and he walked faster to make space between them. After a few more hours, Brewst welcomed them into the city and took them straight to the palace.

After a formal welcome with dressed guards and instruments, Amedeo had them come in and help themselves to a special feast, and to honor Brewst, Amedeo invited all the ones he revealed as powerful to the feast and were seated at the table with them in their new positions at the palace.

After the meal and during the entertainment Brewst leaned over to Mary and spoke. "You must make the first move; he feels like what he did for you will make you feel you owe him and doesn't know that you really love him. I'll stay out of your business, but he is not going to take the first move because of that, the ball is in your court." With that, he got up, grabbed Zen, and walked with Amedeo to his private garden.

To show his friendship before they started about any other topic Zen had Amedeo drop his pants and he healed him. As the three of them stood there after he was done Brewst said "What can I say I didn't expect this guy to be so kinky." Pulling up his pants, Amadeo thanked him repeatedly. "It's okay," Zen said, "but I need a couple of favors. I wanted you to know I am asking in good faith, so I wanted to give to you first before I asked for anything" Zen explained.

"Anything I am at your will," stated Amedeo.

"I'm looking for a ring, it is a gold band with crescent moons carved into it around the band. I have been told by a spirit being it is here, and I need it for my journey. Also, there will be two women who will come pretending they have official business but they are really looking for me. It is okay if you can bring them to me," says Zen.

"I will set you up in our best rooms and treat you all like royalty till we can find what you need," Amedeo responded.

After a few days Zen was sitting in Amedeo's private garden and Mary finally came up with the courage to approach him. She first tries terribly to make some small talk and even ends up on the weather.

"Wow this view huh, the sea is so vast and beautiful," she says trying to find some way of starting a conversation with him. "Can't beat the weather," she says smacking her hands together and grimacing at how poor her start was.

Zen was quite bewildered at her actions and frankly, concerned. "Mary, what is wrong?"

At first, she sat down quietly but also completely flustered and blushing but then jumped to her feet and looked deep into Zen eyes.

"I have feelings for you, and I feel stuck, and I need to tell you even if you don't feel the same," she said sort of trailing off at the end of the sentence.

"I understand, you feel like you want to show appreciation, but it's not needed I know, and thank you," Zen replies.

Mary interjects "That is not it at all," Ugh why was this so hard as tears start to well up in her eyes, "I love you! She spurted out It's more than what you have done for me it's the person you are and-"

At that Amedeo and the rest came rushing in, "We found out. It was in an old mage room that had not been used in years. Here, look is this it?" They excitedly exclaimed to him. As they sort of

94

push past Mary she slowly slinks away and Zen watches her go as they show him the ring.

Mary dropped her shoulders and slowly walked back to her room; 'He doesn't see me, that way,' she thought. How could someone like him be interested in me? He probably just sees me as dirty for what happened. Slowly more and more depressing thoughts raced through her head. She jumps onto her bed and sobs bitterly thinking her love is unwelcome. After a while Duncan busts into her room, she starts to yell at him, but he says to Mary "It's Zen hurry."

When they got back to the garden everyone was just staring as Zen was convulsing on the floor but with a strange red aurora around him. Every time someone tried to touch him the red field would spark them. Mary asks Brewst "What the hell is happening?"

"I have no idea; I don't know what is going on with him," Brewst says.

"Amedeo, we must try to get that ring off him" yelled Duncan. "We are trying but it won't let us, it's like it is protecting him from us." Cat standing behind everyone running his hand through his hair on top of his head, "Wait Mary you try."

She looked at him puzzled, "If it is protecting him from danger, I have a feeling it won't stop you." She got closer and reached out her hand to him while she quietly kept saying 'It's me you are safe; you are safe now.' The rest watched in amazement as her hand went through the field and it dissipated, and he stopped convulsing. Even after this, they could not remove the ring from his finger, so they had Cat pick him up and bring him to his bed. As Cat picked him up, he looked at Mary and said "Good job kid!"

After a couple of hours, the guys came back to the room and asked if there was anything new. Mary, who is sitting on the side of his bed holding his hand, said "No he hasn't moved. Do you think the Ring is killing him?" She asked. "No, no I don't think so, just in the time I haven't seen him to now I can see his power has increased greatly!" Brewst remarked

Well, let's see if anything is better in the morning and they all went off to bed besides Mary. She stayed and no one said anything about it. After a while, she climbed into bed and lay next to him holding him as tight as she could. She kept telling him she had him and he was safe! She fell asleep lying there pretending that he loved her.

The next few days nothing changed till one morning Mary had left just for a moment to wash up, when she came back in, he was sitting up on the side of the bed. She screamed for everyone, "Guys! He got up!" and ran into the room and gave him a big hug. "We thought we lost you," she said. He hugged her back and said, "I'm ok." Everyone came in and told him how happy they were and Amedeo apologized repeatedly for what had happened. Finally, after a lot of commotion, Zen spoke up and said "I really need to use the bathroom."

Soon after he made his way to the table, and they started feeding him. After a while Amedeo's master of the house came into the room and announced that two women were requesting an audience with the High Wizard. Everyone looked at Zen, "It's okay to let them in they are the ones we are waiting for."

Chapter 12

Vannick rode his horse so hard that when he finally reached his master's castle walls the horse died on the spot from exhaustion. He hurriedly walked into the main palace room where Duke Moritz was sitting on his grand throne fashioned to look like Stone skeletons holding him up and with real skulls on the top of it. So, all brought before it would have terrible dread of the man sitting on it.

Report Vannick the Duke demanded.

The watcher has a protector, he called himself the master of elements then hit us with a tornado!

"How are you alive then?" questioned the Duke. "He had us thrown into a lake, so it didn't kill any of us," said Vannick.

"Weakness, maybe we have found a better prize than the old man!" Pondered the Duke.

Vannick explained all that had happened

"Take 3 dozen of our warrior monks, find the master of elements, and see how soft he really is. Do not fail me Vannick I will not be so sweet."

"What about the watcher?" asked Vannick, "Let's kill his protector first and bring the watcher his head!"

Vannick and the warrior monks are known for ruthless fighting skills and dangerous magicians. They set straight for wherever they heard the protector was going.

The two women entered the room after being announced, but Zen was still too weak to stand so he sat there next to the high Wizard. The first one was strikingly tall and dark. Her carved muscle body was that of a true warrior and she carried a long spear with a silver tip that was too large for most men to be able to be wheeled. The second looked as dangerous and she was beautiful and the way she dressed you could tell she was from the far East near the Great Ganges from a people known for trading. Her many different bracelets, jewelry, and chains made her look like a princess.

Divya was very strong-willed and smart. She could read people very well and knew what she wanted in any given situation. She was kind but you had to work to see that side of her.

Amina on the other hand was very strong and a proven warrior. She was born deep in the never-ending forest below the southern desert kingdoms by the coast. Her father gave her as a tribute to his king when she was young, and the king then traded her to merchants from the far east. She was then given to the emperor of a far east island kingdom again for tribute. After which she was trained in many ways of combat but because she won favor and was highly respected by the emperor, she was given her freedom when he died a decade later.

She didn't talk much but when she did it usually was for a specific purpose. She had been hired by Divya's Father a few years ago to protect her and they slowly became very good friends, especially after combating many difficult situations together. They both had been traveling west seeking treasures to bring back home to her village and help grow her father's large trading business by searching out for new cities and opportunities.

The tall one spoke first. "Mistress Divya is the daughter of the grand lord of the Rajasthan province. She has come a long way to find a man who can control the elements. If you will help us, find him, we are willing to give you a handsome reward."

Zen then said, "What is the reward?" Divya walked over to him and put his face in her decorated hand, "Maybe a kiss for you my sweet." at which Mary got out of her seat.

The High Wizard then said, "The man you seek is a friend of ours. Why do you seek him?"

Divya again spoke up saying that he was looking for her and she had something to give him.

She uttered the word both innocently and dirtily at the same time.

"What do you really want from him?" The High Wizard demanded.

Divya then turned to Zen, "You are the man are you not?"

"How do you know?" Zen asked.

"I have a special gift that helps me see the worthy ones and you look very worthy."

With every word, Mary gripped the chair arm and tablecloth tighter and tighter.

The tall woman said, "Stop playing Divya and tell the man."

"Oh, Amina, you take all the fun out of everything."

"I can see you have on the holy breastplate of gold and gems which gives off great protection and truly is one of the most holy relics known to man. The pendent of Boudica, on which the inscription says whoever wears this into battle will have the power their ancestors used in fighting. The ancient ring of Banitu can help amplify different protections for different attacks."

"Oh, and an old silver dagger."

"Do you have any idea how much power these pieces have? Yet you wear them as if you have no idea or care for them," stated Divya.

"I apologize my name is Zen, and you are right I don't know how to properly wear these items but I have been sent here to meet you so you will teach me." After that they all sat down at the table and shared food and each side introduced themselves and told the stories of their journeys and how each of them met however Divya was careful not to allow Zen to touch her. Amina went on to tell him how a bright spirit showed up one night to both and he told them they needed to get to the city by the ocean, Eretria, and look for the High Wizard and he would lead them to a man that can control elements and that Divya would help him and give him a gift. Something he was looking for.

Divya explained that she can see the magic or power in all inanimate objects, and she can help arrange the ones Zen has to provide him with the utmost strength. Every chance she got to say the silver dagger was useless she did as loudly as she could. So, while everyone else had fun getting to know the new two Mary's blood pressure kept rising.

Brewst explained what happened when Zen put the ring on and how since then he has watched Zen's power level go to a place that is hard even for him to read and how Zen is still very weak and can't really stand for himself.

Divya then pulled out of her pocket another ring, "Zen the ring you have is two different rings but when you put them together it will amplify the power of both." Mary interjected, "Maybe now is not the time he hasn't recovered from the first one." That remark made Divya smirk and she slid the second ring up to the first one. As soon as they touched, it was like an explosion that knocked everyone back several feet, the chair under Zen blew apart and he hit the floor, the table behind him slammed into the wall.

This time no convulsion and no field or aurora Zen just lay there as if he was dead. "What the hell was that?" someone yelled. They all rushed to him. They yelled at Divya "What happened? What did you do to him?" Divya started crying, "I don't know, I don't know. Let's get him into the water."

"In the washroom was a very large tub that everyone privately bathes in," Amedeo said.

As Cat picked him up and carried him off to the tub and Amedeo's servants filled it with warm water

"Take his clothes off," Yelled Divya.

"WHAT?" yelled Mary.

"We need to see if his body is bruising, if it is, he is dying but the water should calm him." After following her directions, they tried to take off any of the sacred items but could not even be touched.

After Divya thought it was safe, they dried him and laid him back in his bed. The group then confronted the two women. "What the hell was that Divya?" demanded Amedeo

"Truly I don't know, that should never have happened. From all the ancient knowledge passed down to me never has someone reacted like that. If I had to guess, I would say that these items are awakening something in him. Maybe something even, he had no idea was there."

"Now what?" said Cat, "I guess we are right back to where we started?" The group left the room, letting Zen rest. Mary, however, did not budge.

Divya would come into the room, every now and then to check on Zen and Mary sat there the whole time just staring at her. "Damn, if looks could kill my head would melt coming in here," whines Divya.

For the next two days, he didn't move at all, besides that he was still breathing you might think he was dead. On the second night, Diya came back in and Mary stepped out for a moment to come back in to find Divya sitting in her chair and holding his hand. Mary went into a rage and told Divya that this was all her fault and that she told her that he was weak, and they should wait but her stupid ass wouldn't listen. Divya calmly got up and walked out of the room but turned to Mary on the way out.

"You can hold his hand and beg all you want but he is a true warrior with great power. He will never have time for the likes of you." Just as Divya cleared the door, a vase crashed into the door jam and exploded into a million pieces.

The next day around noon time Zen finally woke up. Mary was there this time and welcomed him back from the dead. He smiled at her "Hi!"

"Hey," she replied with a smile.

"How do you feel?" she asked.

"My head really hurts, can I have some water?" he asked. "Sure" as she ran out of the room to get some and tell everyone. They all came in as well as a sheepish Divya who apologized and begged for forgiveness. "That should have never happened, it just doesn't make sense," she said.

After a while, Zen asked if everyone could leave the room he needed to talk to Divya in private. As Mary slowly walked out of the room feeling defeated and when the door shut it was like her heart broke.

She rested on the wall beside the door biting her lip and trying to fight off a crying face.

"I need you to be honest and explain to me exactly what each thing does here" So she started with the breast plate and went down the line and after she finished, she said "Oh and you have that dagger. Where did you even get that junk?"

Zen went over and picked it up, holding it in his hands. "It is my most prized possession!" holding it up in the sunlight.

"Why?" demanded Divya.

"This is the only way I was able to bring Mary back and give her another shot at life."

After a very long pause between them

"You love her don't you?" she asked.

Zen didn't say anything, he just kept staring at the dagger. She then reached her arm out and said "It is time you touch me."

"Why?" he asked.

"Even before I walked into the room the first time I could feel the Dagger, it is more powerful than all the rest combined but only because it is tied to her heart," Divya explained.

"Why did you act like it was worthless?"

"If you didn't love her, I would have stolen your heart and shown you a truly great life," Divya said flashing her great smile.

"But because it's how you were able to bring her back the dagger is tied to her heart and feelings and that is how it is so powerful, even more than the rest of the items for you due to the connection."

"There are many strong things but very few are stronger and have more power than a women's love. Men can love and many wars and fighting have happened because of it but a woman's heart is built differently."

"Take it from one who knows and knows the power of things. If you hold on to this, it will help you more and more as she comes to love you more and more. You can tell she loves you with all her heart when you see the power radiate from it. That is why you should touch me," Divya explains.

He then touched her and took in all she said. After which she said "I won't get in the way" with a devious smile and left the room. Immediately Mary stormed the room and asked "What that was all about?" But she wouldn't let Zen answer, because she was afraid of what he was going to say. So she proceeded to her next question, "You touched her, didn't you?"

"Yes, I did," which sent Mary into a yelling fit, and stomped out of the room. Just after she got out of the door. She was in the void, "What are we doing here?" she asked. "Let me show you something and if after watching it you're still mad I will let you go," replied Zen. She crossed her arms and huffed.

He said "I learned something new with all this stuff" Just then the stuff on the walls of the void moved and played the whole thing from his eyes. "How did you learn this?" she asked. "I stopped time and played with it for a long time."

"Like how long?" she asked.

"A couple of weeks," I think he replied.

"How often do you do that to us?" She asked.

"A lot!" he said with a big smile.

She stood there and watched the interchange and tears welled up in her eyes. "You love me!" she said as the tears streamed down her face, he grabbed her hand pulled her closer, and softly kissed the tears off her cheeks. She leaned up to kiss him back, but he said "Wait! I don't want the first time to be in here." At that moment she was outside his room and stopped and turned around slowly to face him and they just stayed there for a moment staring at each other.

At that moment the bells started chiming and horns blowing Amedeo and Brewst ran down to Zen room. "Sorry, but those are warnings for raiders." Mary turned to them, "He is still too weak, Zen you can't."

"Guys the Guide came to me these raiders are powerful warrior monks and they won't stop till we are all dead. I must stop them." They all look back at him blankly. At Zen's insistence, Amedeo takes them all down to a basement room that can be defended. He then herded all of them down there and as he was ready to shut the door Cat said "I'm coming with you."

"Cat you can't, you and Amedeo need to stay here with Duncan, and the girls, and protect them." Amina rolled her eyes!

Brewst you have to come with me maybe you can help by taking away their power. Just before locking the door, he stared into Mary's eyes as it shut, and he heard it lock. "I really need to get Cat a weapon. Come on let's go" Zen commanded.

Zen was running to the front door with Brewst in tow. "So, what Is the plan what are we going to do?" "You're not going to do anything you're going stand behind me, but you are the one that was picked by the Guide to watch and tell the others."

"What, that doesn't make any sense" shouted Brewst.

Zen stops for a minute; "I am going be put in spots where I must get rid of threats to the ones, I love but it's all actually a test for you all."

"Huh, what!" Said Brewst

"What you are going to see is going to give you nightmares for the rest of your life. When you tell the others there is a likely chance you all will become afraid of me and leave me." Zen explained.

"There is no way that is going to happen Zen! We will never leave you, Mary is not leaving you if you haven't noticed."

"I wish that was true but when the last Zendaria hit this sort of test. All but one left him and when the next one came, he was alone." As he was explaining to Brewst they got to the front gate. "Open the door and close it behind us. No matter what you hear do not open this door." Zen demanded.

He slowly walked across the draw bridge and as it was Dusk, the sun was already going down so it lit up the evening sky with lots of colors. Vannick standing in front of the sunset by Zen's line of sight Yells "Well if it is not the master of elements. Well, this time I have 3 dozen specially trained magician warriors that have trained to fight for decades. We will not stop till everyone you love is burning."

"Vannick, if you leave now I will allow you all to live but if you refuse your deaths are on you. I have given you all fair warning," Zen says sternly.

Vannick laughs and spits to the side of his horse, "We have a defense all ready for your wind attack boy. These men have decades of training in their gifts and powers. We are going to teach you what power is" he continued.

"What do you want me to do Zen?" asks Brewst,

"Watch and forgive me," Zen replies.

With that Zen stood still and closed his eyes, and his body tensed up and he let out a loud moan and gasp

He reached out his hand fingers fully extended then closed both fists tightly and quickly put them down by his sides.

Slowly the grass beneath the horses dies and then the ground dries out. Then the horses start to buck and try to run but they are stuck to the ground for some reason then the men begin screaming.

First one at a time then all of them. Terrible blood-curdling screams from men and horses alike. At first, Vannick watched in horror but then it started to happen to him. It felt like his entire body was drying out and it hurt immensely. Then Zen aged all of them exceedingly fast, which also brought great pain to Vannick the sheer terror of his last moments.

Brewst screams over the sounds, "What are you doing to them?" but Zen doesn't answer and just keeps his gaze on the fighters. Slowly at first, but then faster and faster the men and horses start to age rapidly. The guards on the wall behind them are scared and frozen.

The horses start to break down and the men fall to the earth rolling in pain as body fluid and blood are squeezed out of their bodies as they twist and turn into dust and just skeletons in armor.

Then it is dead quiet, not a single sound. The guards watching on the wall didn't break out in cheers but were still frozen in fear. Brewst then falls to a seated position trying to wipe the tears from his eyes, "What did you do to them?"

Zen looked down then right at Brewst, "I dried up the water in their bodies and then speeded up the aging processes till only bones were left then I stopped it."

"Suck! That made me empty my bowels Zen," Brewst cried.

Zen reached his hand out and helped his friend up. "I know, I have no excuses. I understand what you must do."

Then over Zen's shoulder appeared two large red glowing eyes about 20 ft up in the air. Zen pulled Brewst to his feet but Brewst was completely mesmerized by the bright red eyes in the sky over the top of the skeletons with the Sun not just set as the backdrop.

"Who are you?" asked a voice from the being with red eyes and an unnaturally deep voice. The bass of the voice made the ground and the stone blocks in the castle walls shake.

"Why do you mask your power from me?" the voice demanded.

Zen turned around and staring up at the glowing red eyes said "I am Zendarian!"

"Impressive Zandarian I have not witnessed that power in a long time maybe we should see how powerful you really are." With that, a giant red outline of the being showed up to show off its sheer size.

"I am a simple human trying to get ready for the test, I apologize if I have offended you," Zen replied. "I only mask my power to show submission and that I know I am weaker than your ranks," he added.

"Prepare well boy you will need it; I look forward to your test," and with that, the being hit Zen with force so hard that it lifted him into the air and shot back the full 20 ft so that he hit the front gate door the wood cracked and then Zen hit the ground.

"NO" screamed Brewst as he ran to his friend, but Zen was not breathing this time. "No God damn it! NO!" he screamed as he pounded on his chest calling for the guards to open the door, they did slowly still terrified. Brewst threw Zen over his shoulder and ran with him as fast as he could back to the palace.

Chapter 13

In the room in the basement, they heard screaming and banging and things falling over. Cat and Amina ready themselves for what comes to that door. Then they hear the screaming getting closer than banging on the door, but the voice is familiar. "God damn it, it's me!" Brewst tells them to open the door.

"Zen is dead!" He manages to wheeze out.

They opened the lock and opened the door. "He isn't breathing. We must help him," and he led them to the body lying on the table upstairs. As they removed his clothes his body was one giant purple bruise. They removed his breastplate and reached for the dagger on his belt. "Wait," Divya said looking at Mary. "That's what is probably keeping him alive leave it."

Holding the breastplate up to the light to inspect it she saw that it didn't have a scratch on it. "This must have also protected him from the blow that was meant to kill him instantly," Divya said holding it.

Amina rushed up to the table and pushed her way to feel Zen's chest and side then plunged a long copper Spike into his chest. The entire group screams "What are you doing!" Ignoring them she pulls it out, and blood pours out of the wound. Zen coughs up a lot of blood but at least he is breathing now. They look at Amina, she smiles and says, "I have a lot of battlefield injury healing experience."

Divya starts searching the Palace with help from the staff looking for any healing artifacts and Amadeo goes to his lab and tries to come up with all the healing potions he can think of.

They meet back at the table with the others. "Here run this on his chest and throat and pour this one on his feet and rub it in Mary." Amedeo instructs.

"Did you find anything Divya?" asked Duncan, but she only shook her head.

"All we can do is wait and pray," says Amedeo, "Let's wrap him up so he is warm and put him in his bed."

Cat picks him up and the girls wrap him up in blankets. He carries him to the bed and puts him down, "Wait, put him on his side so he doesn't choke on the blood he is still coughing up every few moments,"Amina instructs

All of them standing there around him and Duncan turns to Brewst "What the Hell happened out there?" he barks.

Brewst tells them what Zen said on the way there and what happened and how terrible it was to hear and watch and then what happened next till he came and got them. After the full story, he then looked down and said "He told me I would have nightmares for the rest of my life, and I believe him!"

"It was a live nightmare," added Brewst.

They all stayed silent for a while pondering over what had happened. Duncan broke the silence.

"Let me get this straight, Our friend protects us and goes alone, no offense Brewst, to face three dozen of the infamously skilled Nazahera Warrior monks and he knows that to save us he will do something that will make us leave him but does it anyways so he can save us. Is that right?"

"We have all heard of these monks they are trained killers, and they told him they won't stop until we here in this room are burning! What did we want him to do? It didn't scare us when he made these two new bodies or money to pay for stuff or food and clothes, but we are drawing the line here at saving us?" Duncan says.

Cat with his big arms crossed then shouted angrily, "Damn, I am not giving up on him!" Everyone agreed.

After everyone left and went to their rooms, Mary stayed with him and when they were alone, she crawled in bed and laid next to him as close as she could but whenever she touched him, he would moan in his sleep.

This time as she lay there she didn't have to pretend his feelings for her and even though he was so ill she knew in her heart they would have a moment together and lay by him more content than she had ever felt before.

The next morning the Top advisors came in to have an audience with Amedeo, "Sir we have a problem."

"Now what?" he said exasperatedly, "Sir the city is empty."

"What do you mean?" Amedeo asks.

"No one came out of their house this morning, no one. Everyone is terrified at what happened last night and the story is spreading throughout the land like a brushfire. We must do something before fear turns into panic and…," the advisor trails off without finishing his sentence.

Amedeo looks to his right where Brewst is standing, "Only bad will come from this," Brewst admits.

Lady Caihong comes forward. "I could have my ship come to the palace docks and take them all away but to where?"

"Amedeo, I have an old family house on an island a little distance from here, but it is a small island with just fishermen and smugglers we should be able to hide there for a while without being noticed."

"High Wizard I never doubt your judgment, but you cannot leave now. You must stay here and help calm the city and help them forget about Zen," says Lady Caihong

The other advisors agree, "This is no time to leave."

Lady Caihong then leaves to prepare the ship for departure but the preparation takes time and their worst fear comes to life as the masses begin to panic. It was led by an older wizard Hoebrown and some mages under him who spread that Zen was evil and he would start a massive plague in the city killing everyone. Really, he was hoping to take advantage of the situation and unseat Amedeo for his power.

After a few hours, the ship was still not ready and a very large mass of people started to crowd around the palace and demanded Zen be turned over and executed. As time dragged by, they got louder and louder till they started banging on the doors.

Duncan looked worried and stared out at the dock wondering where was that ship.

"Listen we need to buy more time for Zen, so we need to protect the three main entrances if they get breached. Mary, you stay with Zen, Brewst you, I, and Divya will take the courtyard,

Animo you need to cover the back area by the dock and Cat…" he said with a long pause. "You need to go through the front door," said Amedeo.

With no hesitation, Cat made a beeline to the front door telling the boys who worked at the palace who had been struggling to try to keep the door locked, he was coming.

Amedeo yelled, "Try not to kill anyone they are just scared villagers, not killers."

Cat nodded in acknowledgment and then turned to the workers "Open it up boys and close it right behind me."

As the door opened the crowd tried to surge inside till they saw Cat and slowly backed up as a group.

Cat then in a loud voice said "I don't want to hurt anyone but if you think you're getting inside you're coming through me," he said as he pounded his fist into his hand.

A man in the front said, "You don't scare us dog, there are 100s of us." Cat stared at him for a moment then cracked his neck and said, "OK, you first."

He roared and moved towards the man but that freaked the crowd out and they mostly ran for cover and then after a safe distance started throwing things at Cat.

He stood proud with his arms crossed and let it hit him and if something was a bit larger, he smacked it down.

Meanwhile, about a dozen men thought they could sneak in through the back way by the docks until they turned the corner and saw Amina standing there with her spear blocking the hallway and Duncan behind her.

"You boys come to play?" she asked.

A couple of guys pulled out their swords and one said "You don't scare us," as they came forward.

Amina swung her spear around and twirled it in the air above her head then assumed a fighting pose and motioned with her fingers to bring it on.

The first one came in and she easily knocked him out of the way, and she started to twirl again but this time advancing at the men. Easily defeating them and making the ones who could run away while Duncan cheered her on.

Also, the crowd had broken into the courtyard where Amedeo stood and Brewst and Divya were behind him.

The Wizard Hoebrown came in with his men and a crowd behind them. HoeBrown started into a big speech about how Zen was bringing death and plague to the city, and Amedeo was a traitor to the city and its people, and that he also needed to be killed and the palace cleansed bringing the crowd into a frenzy.

Amedeo then said, "If you leave now, I will completely forget this ever happened but if you take the first strike, we will defend ourselves and the consequences are all on you and Hoebrown."

You could feel the tension between the crowd and the three of them. The crowd wanted blood, but no one thought Amedeo was weak. Finally, the mages of the wizard (mages in this part of the world are considered students of a wizard) came and stood at the front and started to move their hands in a way that showed they would attack.

Amedeo said one last time, "I will give you the first strike but that's it."

Brewst turned to Divya and said, "Listen, you better get inside this looks like it's going get ugly quick."

She smiled and a knife dropped from each sleeve to her grasp, "No way am I missing the fun."

Brewst could do nothing but smirk and be impressed.

Just before the fight started Artyom and young Clio came out on the terrace overlooking the courtyard and ready themselves. Aeolus came running out and joined the others in the courtyard and just as he ran in, the Mages set their attacks which were plotted ahead of time so that they would get Amedeo's attention and Hoebrown could fire right after the initial attack hoping to wound Amedeo.

It might have worked but after Amedeo blocked the first few shots Aeolus ran up to block HoeBrown and ran straight at the Mage in front and hit him with as much force and power as he could muster. While the ones with power continued to strike and block each other in the middle everyone else came around the sides so Brewst and Divya got back-to-back and stood in front of the door.

Divya said, "No one gets past us." And Brewst just nodded.

Meanwhile, Artyom and Clio started firing at the crowd but what made them less effective was that they were trying to pull their punches to help slow the crowd for Brewst and Divya. Both fought fiercely and back-to-back they moved through the assailants with grace like they had done this a million times before.

Brewst was good with a sword but being in the fight he couldn't concentrate on taking away anyone's power. Between Brewst and Divya, they made a great effort to fight back the first 30 villagers or so but more just kept coming.

Brewst yelled out "We can't stop them!"

Amedeo then raised his arms in the air and brought them down hard to a clap in front of him releasing a great burst of wind that knocked everyone off their feet. At that moment Artyom did the same to the people behind them trying to get past Brewst and Divya.

Then Clio Looked up at the sky and her hair seemed to turn to a blazing fire. As she was pushing her arms out, Artyom screamed, "Clio NO!" But it was too late, and the full force hit Wizard Hoebrown and turned him instantly to ash along with one of the mages that was close to him. This scared everyone and they all ran away.

Clio hit the ground crying for what she did as that was the first time; she had taken a life. Artyom tried to console her.

After they saw the villagers running away, they all flopped to the ground exhausted.

"I see you are good with that thing," Divya said deviously to Brewst.

Brewst just smiled and raised his eyebrows up and down.

At that Duncan came running in, "Whoa," he said seeing a bunch of injured and the ashes.

"The boat is here, let's get out of here before they come back with more."

They yelled for Cat and everyone ran down to the dock back behind the palace.

Amedeo turns to Brewst, "There is an old man named Hero, he takes care of the house for me. I will send my trusted servant, the master of the house, with you to set up your stay and make sure everything goes as smoothly as possible."

"You have been a great friend; we appreciate all you have done," Brewst replies.

"Amedeo my heart will go with you, please tell Zen that my house is always open to you all and if I can help in any way, please let me know."

Brewst then called the group together, "Listen we have got to get out of the city before it really explodes."

"We can't! Zen has not even regained consciousness yet," responds Mary.

"We can't wait, the city is terrified by last night and they tried once but if that panic builds back up they will tear this place apart," says Brewst.

Cat picked up Zen and everyone gathered their things and made their way down to the docks and waited for the boat to show up.

The boat finally was tied to the dock and all boarded and set sail as fast as they could. Amedeo and his advisors all waved from his private garden as the boat sailed off to the horizon.

"Do you think we will ever see him again?" Cat asked Duncan. "I hope so Cat, I hope so."

As the boat leaves the dock and sets off the tension finally starts to release, and they start to relax.

However, after coming out of a cove and passing into the sea they cleared the last rock wall but there was a boat full of drunk fishermen and other villagers and they rammed their boat straight into the ship. They started to try to climb over onto the ship, but Cat just started picking people up and throwing them into the sea. Again, Brewst and Divya joined in and tried their best not to kill anyone but as Divya would say later a little stabbing was ok. After they finally cleared that and the boat was safe to keep going the final set off for the island.

Chapter 14

Mary, after seeing what the plan was, went to Zen's room and lay next to him saying a small prayer for him to be ok. After a few days the crew said they would make the island the next day so try to make sure they are ready to go as they will have to get you set up and return as fast as they can.

That night the group sat on the deck and looked up at the stars. "What if he doesn't ever wake up," asked Amina.

"Last time we checked he was still bruised everywhere, and you know the regeneration powers he has," she remarked.

"We will give him all the time he needs. He deserves at least that much from us," says Brewst.

Mary went to Zen laying down to face him. She leaned over and gently kissed him silently begging him to please be ok. She fell asleep like that.

The rest of the group slowly each went to their rooms, leaving Brewst and Divya on the deck drinking and trading stories under the stars.

"What was the coolest thing you have ever seen?" Brewst asked her.

"North of where I'm from there is a group of villages we trade with, and the mountains rise high enough above the clouds to look the gods in the eye," she giggled. "They are so majestic and imposing that no ordinary man can climb them, just looking at them from a great distance is awe-inspiring. I always loved going on that trip with my father and his men. He loved having me by his side to share with me the great and wonderful mysteries of our world."

"He sounds like he was a great dad," brewst responded.

"He is." She spoke softly.

"He is so strong and wise, yet he wasn't demanding. The love he had for his little girl was more than his respect for tradition. He would have been more than happy for me to stay there but he wanted me to follow my heart. I know it wasn't easy for him but he gave me the greatest gift a father could give his daughter." The glint in her eye showed how much she admired her father.

"What about you, have you traveled much?" she inquired, taking another sip.

"Oh yes, most of my life actually. I have seen the desert kingdoms in all their glory in the south and swam in the waters on the large, beautiful Nile. I have spent most of the past ten years all over. I have seen more than most people will ever see in two lifetimes but the most beautiful thing I have ever seen are women."

"HA!" Divya blurted out of her mouth; "I think you walked me right into that!"

Brewst smiled deviously and said, "No really I mean it, women are truly wonderfully made, from the depth of their love to the amazing beauty of their bodies and pure compassion. They are clearly God's greatest creation. I dare say no wonder in this world is greater."

Divya bites her lip as she watches the words come out of his mouth.

"Does that usually work on all the other girls?" said Divya with a sly smile.

"Divya, I know you could literally have anyone you want and I'm sure there is a long line waiting for you. I just want you to know I'm here. I am one of them waiting, I hope after all your travels, maybe the last one will lead you back to me someday." Brewst says with a mischievous smile.

As the conversation carried on the distance had slowly closed between them. They both now standing barely a hand's width away from each other.

"Maybe we could travel together?" She suggested shyly.

And with that, she leaned in to kiss him, and he welcomed it. She pulled back after making out for a while, "Amina is in my room," she said as she gazed deep into his eyes.

"Everyone below deck," he said smirking. They stood just below the helm deck out of site from the lone crewman steering.

She giggled as she dove back into another long deep kiss with him. His hand slipped down to untie the wrappings of her dress. His fingertips caressed her body admiring each curve. His kisses reached her neck. He then sat her on the side of the ship railing. So as the Sea roared beneath them, he started kissing her slowly under the full moon. His lips slowly worked their way down exploring all over her body. Both were very experienced when it came to making love, but this would be a night that neither would ever forget.

The next morning, Mary felt groggy and slowly opened her eyes and Zen was there laying staring at her. "Hey," he said.

An electric shot through her body and she could barely contain her excitement but just said "Hi," trying to play it cool.

Each just smiling, and taking in the moment.

"Is it just you and I left?" asked Zen.

"No, everyone is still here no one left," she responded. A tear fell down his cheek and this time she kissed it to make it go away. In a way, he knew they wouldn't leave but he would still need to be careful, even though he knew he had built something special in this group.

They just smiled and as they lay there taking in the moment, she slowly leaned over and kissed him. She got lost in the moment and started to get carried away getting a bit aggressive too. When she heard Zen moan, she backed off a bit and they both laughed as their eyes met and they kept saying sorry to each other repeatedly.

"Who the hell wrapped these blankets? I can hardly breathe," remarks Zen. "Please help me out." After she helped him get dressed, he sat on the edge of the bed and Mary walked over. He took her hand. "I don't want you to feel like you must repay me or anything like that," Zen said.

"You're touching me, you know I don't feel that way. I know you rescued me from a dark prison that no one else could have ever accessed and if not for you I'd still be there. It was the way you did it, being kind came so naturally to you and from the moment I saw you. I just knew," she replied.

"Then when I saw what a gift you gave me in this body my heart sang for the first time in a very long time. I wanted to give that to you," Mary said.

Mary leaned down and they kissed. They let out a lot of deep pent-up passion and the happiness they both felt as they both knew what the other felt and they were both happy with that knowledge. After kissing for a while Zen said, "Not here let's wait for the right time," knowing what Mary was thinking. Everyone was outside on a small boat and Zen still needed to gain his strength from what had just happened. So, with Mary's help, he slowly walked out to great applause from the rest of the group.

This time they were all very proud to tell Zen how they saved him and all that had happened while he was out.

A few hours later they docked on the Island of Casperenta and the master of the house walked them all over to Amedeo's family home. It was a three-story oval house with a roof terrace overlooking the ocean. As they walked up a very dark skin man crowned with bright white hair and beard. He looks like a painting of a benevolent god looking down on his subjects. "Welcome, welcome," he yelled from the roof.

Hero and his daughter Cedella showed them all to their new rooms and the master of the house went back to the boat. They all decided to give the top room to Zen and didn't bother giving Mary one. Hero and his daughter stayed in a small building behind this one so there was enough room for everyone to have one, but it didn't take long for the rest to realize Divya was not staying in hers. At first, this was not a welcome change for Amina, but she realized that they worked well together. Maybe something was in the air because Duncan had immediate sparks with Cedella.

124

Cat carried Zen to the room as he was still too weak to make it up the stairs by himself. After waking up from a nap Mary asked him if he needed anything. He just shook his head no.

"What do you want to do?" She asked him.

"I just want to stare at you for a while." He replied

She smiled and said "OK" very cutely. And did a little twirl for him in her dress. They spent the day talking, her asking about that night, and him trying to explain the best he could. After a while, he said, "I could eat, how about you?" She nodded yes "but I don't think we have anything," she said.

"Well, I'm good for something," he said smilingly and the aroma of freshly baked bread came up the stairs from the kitchen. They heard Cat yell, "YES, Zen is feeling better."

Mary helped him down the stairs and all ate together. At the end of dinner, Zen said, "Tonight you all will be visited by the Guide. He will give you a blessing to each of you for staying with me. You cannot ask for something that will affect someone else's freedom of choice and you can't ask him to hurt anyone and lastly, you can't tell anyone till you get it. So, think about what you would wish for so you will be ready when he comes."

They all bantered back and forth as excited children, joking, talking about wishing for wild and crazy things. Brewst said, "Tomorrow we wake up to a giant giraffe." Although he had never actually seen one, a giraffe or Guide. Later that night the Guide visited each one and asked each one.

"So, Mary, what do you want me to grant you, just name it."

"I know what I want, I want Zen to pass his test."

"I'm sorry Mary, I cannot give that to you, he will have to make many personal choices so you cannot have that."

"Well then, I want him to be 100 times stronger than he is right now so he can beat it."

"What do you want to ask for Cat?" asked the Guide.

"So, if I wished for my own house to be full of gold, I could have it?" he asked.

"Well it can only be one thing but yes if that is what you want, I will grant it for your loyalty."

"Well in that case I know what I want."

"So Brewst what do you want to ask for?" asked the Guide.

"So, giving an infinite number of concubines is out of the question?"

"Yes, I cannot grant someone to you against their free will but I'm sure you could woo them yourself." Said the guide.

"Then I know what I want."Brewst said confidently.

Finally, the Guide came to Zen, "You have a very loyal group here each one of them wished for something for you despite my many explanations as to why that won't work," he said with a smirk on his face. "So, you will wish something for each one." "Do I have to do that now?" asked Zen. "No. On your timetable," responded the Guide.

"I think they are all scared of what happened the other night. That being was large, he swatted me like a bug. I am too small to be able to fight this, I think."

"One thread by itself cannot do much but if you put many together you can make cloth and keep adding and that small cloth can make clothes or a blanket to keep you warm. "The guide said.

"Humans are the same, there are small little dots that they are so small human eye can't see, but you keep piling them on top of each other and finally you end up with YOU," explains the Guide. "Why are you telling me this?" asked Zen.

"All material things are made from God and God is abundant energy so every little dot that makes up you has the power of God in it. So, it may seem small and insignificant, but everything can become something greater, and that way everything is possible with God." The Guide went on to tell Zen what was next and what would happen over the next few weeks so he could prepare himself for the challenges ahead.

The next morning everyone was sitting around the table eating and grinning huge grins at each other. As Zen slowly made his way down to the kitchen he walked, and everyone looked at him. He smiled and let out a little laugh, "Thank you all but the Guide said your wishes are all void."

"What?" They all complain at once! "This is not right," one said "Not fair," said another.

Zen said "It is okay" trying to quiet them all down, "I was told that if he granted all your wishes, I would be stronger than God himself. He said with a laugh So, he will allow me to ask for one for each of you but later in our journey."

"So, all of us asked for something for you, even Brewst?" asked Duncan jokingly.

Brewst interjected, "I was talked into it he said jokingly."

"Yes, all, and I thank all of you for your love," replied Zen.

A few more days passed and Zen was finally gaining his strength back and the bruising had mostly gone away. He was enjoying his time with his new family and the warm sea sun and waters helped revive his soul. Mary and Zen would steal small moments when they could and enjoyed just being around each other. she doted on him and he loved the attention. She was trying to just wait till he got his strength back and finally felt better, but this time helped enhance the love between them immensely.

When Mary was not dotting on Zen she would take time and read a book to Cat and help him understand the deeper meanings of it and life and he loved it. The two of them also took time to get to know each one in the group better. The island had truly become a special place for all of them and Hero and his daughter became part of their family.

Chapter 15

As Zen got stronger Hero told him of a Divine god-like creature that lived at the other end of the island but had the whole island in fear. "He hates humans, and we fear we will do something to bring his wrath on us and when he is in a really foul mood no fish will come close to the island which hurts the fishermen."

So, Zen decided the next morning he would go see this creature with Hero to see if he could bring some peace to everyone as thanks for the hospitality he received. When they got there it was a very old stone building that from the outside appears to have been abandoned for years and was very dirty. As they walked toward the door it opened and there stood a 6 and a half feet tall Naga. Naga has a man-type large body, but he has scales and serpent eyes. His hands are large with long thin fingers and nails are that end of each. He is wearing a strange skin-type coat and pants that give off the smell of death.

For a while he said nothing, they were all sizing each other up, and just as Zen was about to speak, he said, "Are you here to end me Zendarian?"

"No, no I would never hurt anyone if I didn't need to," replied Zen.

"A Zendarian that doesn't hurt anyone...." It said with a laugh. "What do you want then?"

"I was hoping I could have some of your time and see if there was something me or the people of the island could do for you.

The people here fear you and do not want to mistakenly raise your wrath toward them," explained Zen.

"Humans have sufficient reason to fear me," he said as he turned to walk back into his house.

He then turned back around and said, "Come in, I will receive you as an honored guest let us share food. Oh, and the human can come in also."

They all sat down at his table. The house was surprisingly cluttered with all types of things. From weapons to stretched skins to clothes and many pots. He cleared off the table and went and grabbed a very large Gord which was full of what he called water snake wine. As he laughed pouring it, he said "This will knock you guys on your ass."

Zen took a sip and it hit him hard the minute it hit the flesh in his mouth. It felt as if acid was burning his mouth and he had no idea what type of alcohol this was but trying to put his best foot forward, he swallowed and he could feel it hit his stomach.

Coughing terribly Zen asked, "What may we call you?

"My name is not translatable into your language, but you may call me Machitis. Once I had a human friend many centuries ago and that is what he called me."

"Thank Machitis for the hospitality. My name is Zen, and this is Hero".

Zen started to talk but Machitis popped out of his seat and said, "Do you want to see a trick?" Not knowing how to react they both agreed.

Machitis then walked over and held out his arm, "Go ahead Zendarian touch me."

"Are you sure?" Zen asked.

He just nodded back yes to him with a huge grin.

Zen reached out and touched him and nothing happened.

Machitis smacked his hands together, "HA! I still got it." Hero was completely confused as to what happened.

Hero turned and looked to Zen as if asking what happened.

"Nothing," a surprised Zen said, "I didn't gain his experiences nothing."

Machitis sat back down and took a drink very pleased with himself.

"Did you know this island and area is my ancestral home?" Machitis said.

Zen, "No I had no idea."

"It's true," Machitis replied.

"How old are you?" Zen asked.

"Way too old," Machitis replied. "Death is taking its time finding me," he said with a laugh and swig of his drink. "When I was first born your race was still hiding in caves," giggled Machitis

"My race predates the humans and the elves and even back to the time of Ogres, Trolls, Dwarfs, The Nekomata, and even the Mermen before them. But not many of any of us are left nowadays."

"I have met a Nekomata he gave me this medallion," said Zen showing Machitis

"My, you are a worthy guest, I have never known one to give anything to any human," Machitis responded.

Then continued with his thought. "Back then I was told everyone fought yes, but just took what they needed to survive. Unlike humans, humans are like a plague that kills and spreads everywhere. Other races are killers too, but Mankind has perfected it I think," Machitis said.

"The worst humans ever were the Nephilim, they killed my family, but I got them good," Machitis said taking a big drink from his cup and wiping his mouth with his arm

"As you can see none of those bastards are left," Machitis said very smugly.

"Seems like it has always just been fighting with your race, the Persians, Greeks, Romans, Vikings all the same. Now I'm all that is left," he said sadly, taking another drink.

"I have heard that some of my people, the Naga as humans call us, are in the far east but I'm last around here."

He then went to a back room and brought out smoked fish. "Go ahead try this. The seasoning is very ancient but it's spicy," Machitis said handing some to both. Both were very fearful after the alcohol, but this was amazing and so tasty and seem to just melt in their mouths, they ate it up. Machitis watched smiling and was very pleased they liked it.

Zen between bites asked if there was anything he or the islanders could do for him now or in the future. A way to show that they wanted peace or even friendship if possible.

"Humans have nothing I need; I'm not being stubborn, it's just true."

The three then spent the next few hours listening to Machitis tell his stories about his life and the ones he came across. His family and others of his kind and what happened to them. Zen and Hero hung on every word.

In the end, Machitis stood up, put his hand out, and shook both of their hands. He said, "I know humans like that referring to shaking hands."

"In my culture when you have honored guests you must give them a present, I think you humans call it commensurate with the size of the honor," Machitis explained.

"Since a great Zendarian came to my house and shared his time with me I will give you these, 1st your human Hero, if you don't heal his heart, he will die in a few days," Machitis said.

Hero's face went blank.

"How do you know?" Zen asked.

"His blood, I can always hear a human's blood pumping and his does not sound right and that is what that usually means, and I know he means something to you so that is my first gift," Machitis explained.

"Second, remember there are much worse things than dying. Living for nothing is much worse but if you find something /one you love you hold on with both hands and don't let go. If you must die for them, then do. There is no better death than giving your life for the ones you love. Maybe it won't be remembered in your human history, but it is revered on the other side, as the highest honor."

"My third gift is if your humans have a problem or question Hero may come and talk to me about it and I will treat him with just as much respect as I would treat you."

Then getting up he walked and moved a bunch of stuff and pulled up a very ornate carved wooden box. And he set it on the table and pulled out a long green crystal. "If you want to know more about the past Zendarian then go south to the other side of the sea, to a place called Cyrenaica, and ask the locals for The Aleankabut Aleimlaq. They will point you to her. She can be trusted but don't go alone and be careful who you bring."

"She is the most ancient being I know exists; she has dealt with many of your kind. You will know you're in the right place because there will be three mountains and between them and the sea is a very lush forest with many plants and creatures but on the other side there is a desert further than the eye can see. As you get closer the crystal will glow brightly and will be a sign for her not to kill you immediately."

"Don't bring any human weapons at all she will be insulted and kill you all. Even you Zen if she wants, she can kill you. But I think she will like you and tell her I sent you."

"There is no way we can repay your generosity," Zen said. "Is there anything we can do?"

"Maybe come and visit and share food and talk, sometimes even for me these same 4 walls just remind you that you're alone. I would enjoy a visit from you or your friend." Machitis said.

At that point, it was night, and the two left to go back to the house. On the way back, Zen healed Hero and he felt so much better and all of a sudden had energy. "Thank you, Zen, and thank you for today," said Hero

"You deserve it," Zen replied, and they both walked home in silence thinking about the day.

That night they told everyone what had happened and that tomorrow he was getting a boat and going to Cyrenaica. Mary objected as she felt he needed to rest and didn't like the idea of him going without her. But Zen calmed her down and told her he needed her here in a place where she was safe.

Since Hero was familiar with the people and area, he, Zen, Brewst, and Cat boarded a ship and set sail for the other side of the sea early next morning.

When they got to Cyrenaica, they started asking the locals for a woman named The Aleankabut Aleimlaq

Everyone was extremely fearful as soon as they heard the name, and some would even run away. Finally, they found someone who for some money took them on camel back to the area they wanted to go. Brewst and Hero stayed back and got them all a place to stay and got an idea of the land just in case.

When Zen and Cat got to the area the man said "They would have to go the rest on foot." With that, he turned around and left as soon as he could.

"Well, I guess that's why we have the crystal," Zen pulled it out and started walking till the crystal got brighter and brighter. Slowly they walked until they finally arrived at a very large hole in the side of the mountain. Foul and dusty air came out in bursts from inside making them both cough. No sane man would venture into a place that smelled so foul, but they went in anyway.

Zen didn't want to use magic in case it would make her mad, so the only light source was from the now bright glowing green crystal. What kind of person lives in a dark dirty cave Zen thought when they heard something move in the dark. Then it moved again, and Cat moaned, "What the hell is that?"

They could tell it was large but not sure how large. So Zen pulled himself together and walked with Crystal out toward the noise. The light from the Crystal illuminated the large figure whose presence they both felt. A massive 12 ft tall spider was staring right at them both and Cat screamed.

The Spider then started to speak but neither of them understood it at all.

After it finished, Zen said, "I'm Zendaria and Machitis has sent me to you for wisdom if I may win your favor."

The spider just stared at them and then walked up to Zen so close the hairs on her Chelicerae brushed up on his face, but he didn't move. He didn't even change his breathing pattern. He wanted to show he was brave even though he knew what Machitis said about her ability to kill him.

The Massive spider then shook the dust off itself and murmured at first then said, "It takes me a moment to remember your language."

"So Machitis sent you? Did you kill him?" she asked.

"No, no he is a friend. He said you know all about the ones like me that came before and maybe could help me with my test. He gave me this crystal to find you." Zen replied.

"I'm glad he still lives." She said, "We fought together against the Nephilim many, many years ago."

"What do you want to know about Zendaria?" she asked.

"Who was the best how can I improve like them?" Zen asked.

"Best by what measure? The best at what?" She replied.

"I guess ones that were successful and how I might pass my test and be like them?" Zen Asked

"Test, how to pass I can't say," she replied.

OF all there were, there were three that stood above the others," she went on to explain. "One was from the Far East and perfected using horses in battle and grew a massive empire that led to many advances in civilization. Another one near here and she taught your kind the stars and how that all worked and many advances in eating and medicine which was the start of the great Desert Kingdoms and they dominated power on earth for a long time."

"But I would say the best is the one who helped your race leave caves and learned how to plant and trade with the Elves and other species. You started to build dwellings which led to your whole civilization. However, my personal favorite was the one who led the last-ditch effort to save mankind from the Nephilim, those were some epic battles."

"What made them successful? ask Zen.

"I just told you," she replied.

"No what about them as people helped them to succeed in these ways," asks Zen.

"They had a sense of love for your species that burned bright, this guided them I think to success." She replied.

"How do you know all this?" Zen asked

"There are many beings on this planet both here and in the spirit side that are a treasure trove of information, but humans look down on anything not human, and the value gets lost to them." She explained.

"What should I call you?" Zen asked.

"To humans, I'm The Aleankabut Aleimlaq, my real name means nothing to you." She spoke.

"I will tell you I'm not sure if I'm on some cosmic quest list, but every single Zendrian has come to me and to be honest most are better prepared at what they are looking for. You are looking for enlightenment and I can give it to you but there is a cost," she said.

"What is that and what is the cost?"

"Well, I bite you and put just a little venom into your system and you will have an Enlighted moment but to get that you must go and get me 100 Cattle. I don't want ones you make the blood doesn't have the same taste and I will know the difference," She spoke.

"Have you ever eaten a Zendarian," ask Zen sheepishly?

She sort of giggled, "Well yes, I have but just one, and, in my defense, he was a jerk. He thought he could force me to comply. So, I made sure I could see his face in my web while the venom turned his insides into slush," she said very pleased with herself.

"You are wondering how you can trust me to not just eat you," she asks.

Zen didn't say anything for a moment and said, "The thought crossed my mind. How can I trust what I see in this vision or enlightenment, is it real?"

"Why are you here?" she asked.

"Because Machitis sent me here and that you could help me," he replied.

"And you trust him?" she asked.

"Yes, yes, I do!" he said.

"What did he say about me?" she asked.

"He said I can trust you but don't go alone."

"Well here comes that part you will leave your friend here with me, so I know you're coming back," she says.

Cat said "OHHH" moaning very loudly.

"There is a Sultan who has a palace not far from here, he has the cattle I desire. You can get them for me, and I will give you what you want," she said.

"You give me your word you will not harm him at all," Zen demanded.

"I give you my word, plus I haven't had anyone to play Mancala with, in ages. He is safe." she said.

Cat gave Zen a frowning face and said, "Please hurry."

Zen headed back to get brewst and Hero and find the Sultan.

Chapter 16

The next morning Hero took the others to the palace gate and in Arabic explained who Zen was and why they needed an immediate audience with the Sultan. After being let in they were asked to stay in a room till called to be brought before the Sultan. The palace was exquisite and all white marble which with the background of sand and the river made it stand out like a jewel even more.

As they were announced he had no idea what anyone was saying until he heard Master of Elements

As they stood before the Sultan, Hero again spoke for the group and Brewst leaned over and said, "We Should have brought Duncan."

Zen asked, "Do you feel anyone?"

"Not in the building but around it," Brewst replied.

Then the Sultam dismissed everyone, and all left except the attendant to his right.

"Please approach." Said the attendant in their language.

"My name is Osman and this the Sultan Idris al-Mahdi al-Muhammad."

The Sultan then said," It is a great honor that the Master of Elements has visited me and my kingdom. What is your ask?"

"I need to trade 100 cattle with you," Zen said.

"Let me guess it's that wicked Spider again," the Sultan said.

"She is an extortionist, have you ever seen her run across a field or jump on something, ugh stuff of nightmares," the Sultan lamented. "So why the trade?" Sultan asked.

"She will not take mine, but I have 100 Cattle at this trading stable in your coastal trading port. She says yours tastes better, so I need to trade to get my friend back," Zen explained.

"Oh God 100 cattle you think she is going have babies again?" the Sultan groaned asking Osman.

"Fine, I will arrange the trade and help you get them out to her, but I need something in return," the Sultan said.

"There is what you would call a wizard outside of my city by the ocean. He is unnaturally old and has been there as long as anyone can remember. His name is Abd al-Malik ibn Marwan. My people feel that he is evil. Bad things have been happening recently and people are demanding something be done. Can you go out there and talk to him? See if you think he is evil, if he is maybe, you could kill him for us?" the Sultan asked.

"I will not hurt anyone unless I must, but I will go talk to him," Zen says.

"Fine. One of your men can go with my men getting the cattle out that way and wait for you. Your other man can go with you since he can speak the local language," the Sultan said. "Zen and Hero, please leave right away with Osman to go see the wizard."

As they got to the wizard's house the door was open and a voice said, "Please, please come in." to Zen and his companions.

Osman refused but Zen and Hero went in, and the old man greeted them, "Oh finally! I have waited so long for this moment."

The old man was sitting in an old wooden chair. He was too weak to get up but greeted them as warmly as he could. His house was so dusty it looked like no one had moved anything in decades, just a small path to the back where his kitchen, bathroom, and bedroom were.

Zen said, "Do you know who we are?"

"Yes, yes of course I have been dreaming about this for decades!" he replied.

"You see I was granted a vision," he started.

"Vision from who?" Zen asked.

"From The Aleankabut Aleimlaq many years ago. In that vision, it said I would not die until I met a Zendarian."

"Oh, I have waited for you for so many years," he said sort of exasperatedly.

"What else was in your vision?" Zen asked

Abd said, "I saw your power, it is a supernatural being that has never been given to anything materialized before. It will reach new heights with you because it loves you and refuses to disappoint you." The wizard was starting to get more and more worked up with every word he uttered.

"I understand trying to settle the very old man down," Zen says.

"NO, no you don't! You must trust it! Completely! You must know it will do whatever it must not to lose you. Trust it," he yelled. Then he turned his head as if to just look down for a moment and fell asleep in death.

Hero turned to Zen with a shocked face, his jaw hanging loose, "Is this what your every day is like?"

Zen replied, "Something like that."

They came out and told Osman that the old man had died but Zen didn't kill him. They parted ways with Osman who headed back to the Sultan and Zen and Hero to meet up with Brewst.

When they met up with Brewst, they saw a bunch of the Sultan's men driving the cattle to the mountain area. The spider had them drive them into another cave on another mountain and once the cattle was in, it put up a web on the entrance so they couldn't get out. The moment the men saw the spider they ran screaming.

Hero just stood there still in shock. "Oh my Holy God!" was all he could mutter.

When she was done with her web Zen said, "You didn't even want the cattle you wanted to prove to me That what I might see is real."

"Clever boy!" she said. "But I did want the cattle, so just think of it as a planned feast," she giggled. "Your friends can come in I won't hurt them."

They all walked over to the cave where Cat was sitting at a massive strange-looking wooden table playing Mancala.

"Hey guys!" Cat shouted. "This game is really addictive!"

As they walked into the cave, "So you know your friends will be waiting here for you to wake up," she said.

"How long will it take?" Zen asked.

"Who knows?" she said "Minutes, hours it depends on the person really," she said.

"Will I ever see you again?" Zen asked.

"That is very doubtful young Zandarian but if you survive and someday are in need of an ally, you may call on me and I will help," she told him.

"How will I call you?" he asked.

"After I bite you, we will always be connected," she said.

She then motioned like something was at the door of the cave and when Zen turned to look, she bit him. Doing so when he wasn't expecting it was the most effective way to get the venom in and he went right out.

At first, all he saw was fuzzy white light then a figure started to walk closer to him and now stood only a few feet away.

"What form would you like I wonder," the figure said.

Zen was still trying to focus when he saw what looked like a gold man standing in front of him, then it turned into his mother, then the guide but it stopped at Mary.

"I see this is your favorite form, I have come to help you, Zen what is it you want to ask?"

"Who are you?" Zen asked.

"Does it matter? Just ask your question."

"How can I succeed? I want to pass my test," Zen asked.

"Succeed? Have you ever thought about what that really means?" It asked. "Who really defines if you succeed or fail? Some random person that doesn't know you or you yourself?" It speaks.

"I want to live and pass my test isn't that success?" Zen asked.

"Let me ask you would you die for her, this form I'm in?" and then Zen's friends appeared behind Mary. "Would you die for them, would that be failing?" It asked.

"You can't worry about what others think might be failing or succeeding, you just need to find out who you are and stick with that and if you are truly yourself, haven't you succeeded?" It asked.

"Who are you Zen? What makes you, you?" It asked.

"I care and I want to be there for the ones I love, and I will do anything I can to be there for them," Zen said.

"Then that is how you succeed! So do what you know is the right thing to do and stick to your own heart even if the consequence for that is death, own it and realize it will be a great death."

As it finishes the sentence things get all fuzzy and then black.

When Zen woke up, he felt very groggy. The bite was still extremely sore so he slowly sat up rubbing his shoulder and saw all his friends were playing Mancala.

"Hey he is up," Brewst said.

"How long was I out?" Zen asked.

"A few hours but sounded like you got a good sleep. You see stuff?" Cat asked.

146

"Yeah, I did but I need time to think about it," Zen replied.

"Cat is right this game is addicting, I would steal it, but I don't want to wake up to a giant pissed-off spider looking down on me." Said Brewst cutting the tension as they all laughed.

They all slowly made their way home.

He was so glad to get back to Mary and he told her all about what had happened and explained in detail how scary the spider was. That night they all ate together and shared the past few days. Zen could not completely focus on what they all were talking about as he kept thinking of his vision and the worry about his test faded. Now it didn't matter as much as being there for them and he knew he could do that.

He spent that next day looking for a boat with Duncan and Hero that they could rent to get to the mainland again to the port city of Izmir and get the last artifact he was told to collect.

While Hero was working out the details for the passage they would have to make. Zen turned to Duncan, "If you need to stay, we all will understand," he said.

"No, I'm seeing this to the end, my friend," Duncan responded.

"Did you ask her to come?" asked Zen.

"Hero is a great man, but he is old, and she won't leave him, she is a very good girl, but I did ask," Duncan said with a weak smile.

Both watch Hero talk to the ship merchant as they talk.

"I just told her I will be back! Let's just make sure we come back," said Duncan.

Zen just nodded his head yes.

After that, they came home and called everyone together for a meeting.

Chapter 17

"We are going to stay here for ten more days. After that, we are headed for the port city of Izmir to look for the last artifact. Which is a rare crystal that has a volcanic rock for a handle or base."

"Wait, you said there would be 5 of us and you have 5 artifacts, is this an extra one?" asked Duncan.

"No, it Is the fifth one the breastplate was never mentioned it just happened and there are actually only four of you and two great additions," explained Zen. "Mary and Amina joined us, but the Guide never mentioned that either of them would," Zen said.

"So, we are leaving them behind then," Brewst said jokingly as Amina punched him in the arm, "Ouch," he said holding it.

Zen then went over a map that Hero had gotten them with the boys to try explaining where they would try to go until it started to get late in the day. After he was done, he looked around but didn't see Mary at all. So, he went up to his room to see if she was there, but she was not, so he went up to the roof. "There you are! What are you doing up here?" asked Zen.

"Just watching the stars and listening to the ocean, thank you Zen for this life. I never imagined I would see or experience any of this, even before."

Mary sat up at the edge of the table as he walked over to her.He could feel the heat radiating from her so, he pressed up closer to her without breaking eye contact. She bit her bottom lip as he leaned in, and they started passionately kissing. Her tongue slipped into his mouth. It intensified as both their tongues danced along each other. He slowly pulled her dress up over her head. He stepped back for a moment to soak in her beauty. "Wow, Babe! Wow! A masterpiece!" he proclaims while taking off his pants.

He climbs up on the table and lies on top of her She lays down as he climbs on top. He hovers over her staring into her eyes. "Do you want to do this?" He asked. She nodded yes and groaned slightly. Playing with her body with his tongue trying to get a reaction out of her. Of course, since he was touching her, he was getting a second-by-second feel of how she felt, and it helped guide him to be gentle and understand what she wanted and needed.

He started kissing her and as it got more heated he stared into her eyes, and he rubbed himself against her. He asked her if she was ready. "Please," she softly moaned, and they took each other's virginity . He helped her through the pain and then slowly made love to each other. Peering into each other's eyes intimately she climaxes and then he does following after her. After which he rolled over lying next to her on the table in the darkness with only the stars above. He held her as tight as he could, "I love you, Mary. Thank you for loving me."

"You're welcome," she responded cutely.

Neither dared talk about the future as they were less than certain they would get one together. They just tried to enjoy the moment and take it all in.

She then said I heard you have superhuman rejuvenating powers and giggled as she climbed on top of him. For the next few hours, it was not some wild brothel fantasy but sweet innocent love that vastly deepened the love and more importantly the connection they shared. They spent the time pleasuring each other in any way they could think of and then falling asleep holding each other under the stars. Over the time they had left on this island the two of them just loved and made love with each other and enjoyed being young and happy.

They all spent time playing in the ocean and walking around the Island. Zen even took the time to take Mary over to the other side of the island to meet Machitis.

On the last night there, they told everyone they were going to have a small wedding service presided over by Hero. Even Machitis who rarely ever left his place came to celebrate.

In her culture way back, the green jade gemstone was considered the most precious and its value was uncountable for the few that had some. So, Zen made her a solid jade ring for her, and they celebrated their love with the new family they had found. As the sun set on that last night Zen sat on the side of the roof terrace watching them all dance. Listening to Hero and his friends playing music and watching his wife twirl around like there were no cares in the world with the sun going down over the sea, it was maybe the best moment of his life he thought. He finally felt like he knew who he was thanks to the love and friendship from this group. He felt he could be open with them and that they would still accept him. Each one of them had helped him love and trust and that made him stronger than he realized.

He then thought about a future where Mary came to him and told him he would be a father and how wonderful that must feel. Watching her be a great mom would be a pleasure. But he stopped himself there and thought let's just enjoy the moment we have instead of the ones we might not get. After the festivities, the night they spent together that night was perfect for both of them.

The next day found them on the boat headed toward the port city of Izmir. They landed excited, healthy, and ready for this new adventure. Hero stayed with the boat and off the others trekked to the port city of Izmir where there was a temple with the artifact they needed.

As they made their way to the temple Zen as always stayed in the back taking it all in but this time holding Mary's hand and feeling like this was where he belonged. There was a large coastal city with a large market and many signs for Gohag, a great merchant in the area renowed for having rare items. They would have to travel through the city, come out the other side to the foot of a mountain where the temple was.

It took two hours to get to the temple, but two guards stopped them at its doors. "No foreigners allowed!"

"Now what?" Duncan asked.

Divya gets ready and Zen freezes time and walks into the temple. He opens a void over the object and brings Divya in too. "Hey, this is new," she remarks. "Yeah, I just picked it up but it is limited, as in bringing a person in is. "Is this it?"

"No, that's a fake it has no energy either," she says.

Ok and next she knows she is outside the temple and Zen says "Brewst you and Duncan go find us a place to stay. The rest of us are going to see someone." "Who?" asked Mary. "The guy on all those signs back there."

"What did the Guide tell you about finding this one?" asked Divya.

"He said it would not be where it should be, but we looked anyway to find where it could be," Zen said.

"Are you Gohag?" Zen asks walking into a small shop. "Why yes, I am friend. What can I do for you?" he responds. Zen then explains what he is looking for saying the one at the temple is fake and he needs the real one. "You are in Luck I just happen to have that item."

"You do realize we can tell if it's a fake or not?"Zen asks.

"Everyone thinks that but only a professional eye can tell," he responds.

"Unless you are an Aito, we are renowned for our ability to see the power link to objects. I can tell if it is fake or not," says Divya. "I just remembered I don't actually have that piece, but I know where you can get it," proclaims Gohag.

Gohag closes the shop and says, "What is in it for me if I help you get it?"

Zen says, "Whatever you wish I will pay. Whatever you like,"

"Whatever?" asks Gohag

"Like whatever as in one thing," Zen responds.

"Ok, ok I just want to know the ground rules here," Gohag states.

"We must travel one day on foot or by cart if you wish, to a town called Kildow, it is famous for having all sorts of artifacts and I know the dealer who has what you're looking for. It is a gorgeous little town right by a huge lake. Meet me here in the morning and we can go together."

They went and met the rest of the group and went to the inn where Brewst had gotten some rooms for them.

They left early the next day and got there still mid-morning but as they were walking into the town the earth was hit by a mighty shake. "What was that?" Duncan said, "I don't like it."

"I think it's the volcano," said Amina.

"Let's get this thing and get out of here," Zen said.

They hurried to the place. Gohag said the crystal should be here. It was a very well-guarded building that housed all sorts of antiques. As they started looking around Gohag went to find the owner and explain what they needed. While walking around again a massive shake but the people here seemed unfazed. "Excuse me," asked Mary, "aren't you all alarmed about the volcano?"

"No, it always does that sometimes more than others, but it's been doing it for almost a year," said a few shoppers. Then another one nodded in agreement.

The next shake felt different, it felt as if something under the ground had snapped.

Zen says "That's it, let's go everyone! Outside!"

The volcano was smoking heavily at that point.

"If this blows there is no way, we can get out of its way," yells Cat over the rumbling.

"Ok see those rocks over that way run as fast as you can for them," Zen shouted.

There was a wall of large rocks they could try to hide behind, but it would not save them from an eruption and the Ash and gas shock wave that would come out if the volcano erupted. But at least puts the city between them and the ocean. So, if it blew toward the city we might survive. Just then a different deeper rumbling started, and Zen stopped as the rest kept running just managing to reach the rocks as the volcano released all of its fury.

The top of the mountain had blown off completely and was shot a half mile into the air, arching right at them. The quake after the explosion knocked everyone off their feet. Zen watched for a few seconds then turned and saw the horror on his friends' faces.

Zen immediately froze time and tried to think. He felt like such a fool for just walking into this situation. Yes, he could control elements but he had to try to think how his powers could be used here. He simply didn't know how volcanos worked so he'd never thought of the different ways he could use his powers to stop one from exploding, if he could that is. And even if he could, was he powerful enough to stop something that large?

He sat there for a while trying to think his way out of this. There must be something. He thought maybe he could make it all just disappear and dematerialize but since he had frozen time, he couldn't use his powers, and he would only have about a few seconds before the volcano erupted after unfreezing time. There was simply no space for trial and error for if he failed, everyone would die.

He'd talked some big talk about protecting them always and now he had put them all in danger simply because he was too engrossed in the idea of getting all the objects. He'd put his family in danger.

After trying to think of any way around this, he realized that if nothing else he wanted to spend the last moments with all of them.

Chapter 18

The next thing he knew he had brought them into the void. Everyone was very terrified, "What can we do?" asked Divya.

Cat shook his head "Nothing," he softly said.

Mary looked straight at Zen, "Can you shield us?"

"I cannot think of any sort of shield that will withstand that. We are either going to be crushed or vaporized," Zen said trailing off.

"Can you somehow make it all stop like that storm on the sea?" asked Duncan looking at Zen but he just shook his head.

Amina asked, "Can you move us while you stop time?"

"No, I can't," Zen replied.

Duncan then said, "But you can run, right?"

"Yes, I can," Zen said very quietly.

"Well, you run then! You run and get out of the blast radius. You have a bigger purpose, you must go on even if it's without us," Mary said as calmly as she could tearing up.

"I'm not going to leave you all," Zen said.

"It's okay Zen, this time we get to save you. You're not letting us down; we are saving you," Cat Said

Zen flopped down to the seat position on the ground and Mary came over and held him as tight as she could.

"How long can you hold this?" Brewst asked. Divya came over and put her arms around him.

"I have been in here for as long as a year. I think you sort of lose track of time, but I can't hold all of you in here for more than a few minutes," Zen explained.

"Then that settles it, thank you Zen for all that you have given us," Duncan says. "The past year was the best part of my life. I got to go on the greatest of adventures and I can go out on a high note, please just tell Cedella I did everything I could to get back to her."

Brewst then said, "It has been the honor of my life to be your friend, all those years I wondered who you were but meeting you has blown away all expectations. Every one of you blew away my expectations," hugging Divya and giving her a small kiss on her head.

"I had nothing before you, just a nightmare existed, you already saved me, thank you," Cat said.

"Sorry I was a pain in the ass, you both are just too cute to not mess with. I'm sorry this is the end I would have liked more time with you all," looking up at Brewst Divya said.

"I am a woman of few words, I like actions, they tell a lot about people. It was an honor to see you in action Zen. I hope you pass your test. When you do remember us," Amina says with a smile.

He then turned to look at Mary at his side and he said to her, "We did not have enough time!"

She said with a smile, "No matter how long it is, it will never be enough!"

"What can you do? What could possibly overpower a volcano?" Duncan says to himself staring at the wall of the void at the exploded mountain.

"You would need God itself to make it stop," Brewst says.

Staring into Mary's eyes, "The power of God…" Zen whispers.

"What?" the group asks together

"I'm going to go back. As soon as we do get on the ground behind the rocks the best you can and try to lay very flat. I will only have seconds. Either I pull this off, which is a long shot, and even then it could still go wrong and kill us all, or I can't pull it off and the volcano does," Zen explains.

Mary said with a kiss, "We trust you; our lives are in your hands, and I can't think of a better place."

When they came back Zen got down on one knee and concentrated on what he was trying to do but he had no idea how it would actually work. He had no idea how the body was built, tiny dots, he could not even fathom what that meant. He thought about making stuff and it just happened. He took the details for granted and now it was going to cost their lives. A Holy Writing verse that the old priest had touched on just came to mind at that moment.

From Holy Writings, "The Powerful Spirit will aid us when we are weakened. And when our thoughts abandon us, and we are unsure of what we should speak, the Spirit understands our pleas for help. It will go forth to the all-powerful God, and He will comfort us and give us what we need."

However, his power knew how it all worked and how to interact with cells and atoms. It did it all the time for him and it did not want to let him down.

As Brewst said, "Someone's power is its own person and can fall in love with its host and when that happens not much can stop them."

Zen never thought about it, but his power was also there the whole time and saw the hole in him even despite the power and watched him grow and find love and a family who would love him for him. As he felt more secure in himself and who he was, his power followed suit. It would now do anything it could to save the one it loved the most, Zen. He had to, in this moment, put his full trust and faith in his power and knew it would come through. Although he had never seen or felt the force inside of him or was ever able to communicate with it, right now he felt his connection to it.

Zen tried to imagine what would happen but in a split second, a force that had never been released in human existence shot out from him sideways at an angle toward the volcano. Somehow his power was able to stop the blast coming back at them but full force just forward.

A giant mushroom cloud shot out from him, and the blast wave was so intense. Not only did it completely blow the Volcano into the ocean but also cut out a half mile down of pure rock and the sea flooded the area where the Volcano was and the lava still bubbling. The blast blew anything above them way up into the upper atmosphere, so it burned up on reentry.

His magic broke that small Atom one of those tiny dots and released the power of God. He tried to aim it but there was no aiming a gun that big, but he saved his friends by trying to angle the blast that took out half of the town but saved at least the rest. The blast knocked out all living things for a while in a few miles' radius.

After a while Cat woke up, he was the first to stir and slowly stand up. "Oh my God!" Cat gasped staring and seeing the ocean where the mountain was before they all passed out. 'What did he do?' he thought. He turned and started to look around for Zen, but he was nowhere to be found. Slowly the rest of the group got up and marveled at how the scenery had changed.

"God Damn it! He did it!" Brewst cried out and started to do a little dance on what was left of the rock barrier they hid behind. But it didn't take long for them to realize Zen was gone. Simply nothing left.

Slowly Mary got up and yelled over to Brewst, "Do you feel him? Brewst I said do you feel him?"

Brewst stopped for a moment and panned around. "No Mary, I can't feel him at all," he said.

Mary started to hyperventilate, and her breathing became erratic as if she was about to faint. Divya and Amina grabbed her before she fell and held her as Mary slowly pulled to and out of the fog of shock, she was in.

"Mary he had every chance to run and save himself, but you knew he wouldn't do it," said Divya. "He gave his life for us, his family for you, his love." Mary fell to the ground and sobbed. Divya just held her, and Amina held both of them and all cried together.

The group just stayed in a state of shock not really knowing what to do or where to go. They all just sort of sat around trying to wrap their heads around that Zen was gone.

After an hour or so a bunch of men on horses came up over the ridge and came down toward them.

"What are the chances this is not bad and they are coming to help?" Duncan opined.

Chapter 19

"My God what happened here?" a man dressed in black in the middle yelled out. "Wow! My day gets better and better. Tell me your savior blew himself up," he said laughing.

"Who are you supposed to be?" yelled Duncan.

"Oh, I'm sorry I'm Duke Mortiz," he said.

"….Mortiz," said Brewst at the same time.

"Oh, so you have heard of me I'm flattered I do seem to fan admirers all over," jeered the Duke.

The Duke is said to have been born evil but even if he wasn't he started very young. First, he hurt animals then moved to the servants and then his three sisters. He murdered his parents when he was 15 and took over the household. He was kicked out of the king's court at 23 for having daily executions and making Artwork with the blood and body pieces but he already had scared his way to being a duke. He is vicious and bloodthirsty but as he got older, he became more extravagant about showing it. Everyone knows it was just best to stay out of his line of sight.

"What do you want?" demanded Cat.

"Well, you see I came to have a good old-fashioned showdown with your master of elements but since he has left us, I'm going to take my aggression out on you all," the Duke said laughing.

Cat let out a mighty roar.

"Whoa! Impressive," said Mortiz smilingly. "Someone's got some fight in him!"

Divya and Duncan both say, "Cat no!"

But Cat screamed, "Protect them, that is what he said, Cat protect them. Brewst do your thing." With that, he started to run toward the men.

"UGH, ok go get them, boys," the Duke said to his warrior monks.

But they were not ready for Cat. He punches the first guy and dodges the next guy's sword, breaks his arm, and then punches him in the side of the head. He then slams him down, picks up his helmet, and beats the next guy with it. He picks up a sword and throws it like an axe into another guy's chest. Grabs the nearest guy and throws him head over heels backwards a few feet.

Amina started to fight them also in a style that was taught to her in the Far East as neither of them had any weapons on them. Amina took a weapon from the first guy she beat and fought them off with that.

Cat viciously battles through a dozen men, and he has released all the anger and rage that has been in him for many years. They were going to pay for having him release it! Then he broke the arm of a man who stabbed him in the back and then ripped his arm off his body and started beating him with it. The monk beyond that scream forget this crap and ran off into the woods.

"Damn, did you see that? Ha-ha, good help is hard to find I'll tell you. Wait did he just say crap?" joked the Duke.

The rest of his men slowly backed up toward the Duke, Cat stood there bleeding from everywhere breathing heaving muscles still rippling, glistening with dirt, blood, and sweat. Cat again let out a mighty Roar and started to charge.

"Okay that's enough!" said the Duke as he raised his hand in the air and pulled it down a bolt of lightning came out of the now cloudy sky and hit Cat in the head, and he fell immediately. Everyone behind him screamed.

The Duke did a little dance and said "Did you see that? Dam that was cool! What a hit! Right on the forehead. You know that is not that easy," he said to the guy to his left.

"Now are we going to do this the hard way or easy?" A horse carrying a cage cart behind started to come down from the ridge. "You all? You are getting into this cart either on your own or in pieces."

The rest of the group looked at each other and slowly walked over to the cart. Duncan turned to Brewst, "What the hell happened?" asked Duncan. "I'm sorry I had the monk's power, but I could not grab the Dukes."

"Is his power like Zen's, where it wouldn't let you?" Duncan asked.

"No, it's more like it is slippery I just could not hold on to it. I'm sorry I let all of you down, I let Cat down," Brewst said with a heavy heart. As they started back up the hill back to the Duke's castle one guy said, "What about the big man?" The duke, slowly passing the cage with everyone in it, says, "Birds must eat. Oops!

Too soon!" he broke out laughing while looking at them. After riding for several hours, they finally stopped and set up camp.

After eating and getting ready for the next day the Duke walked over to the cart. "Hey, I know everyone's down in the dumps and giving up on life I get it, but I must admit I am fascinated with your man," he happened to be looking at Mary when he said that, but he didn't know. "Please tell me about him, I mean in a short period of time he pulled off some amazing stuff! What he did to Vannick, WOW! That man was legendary. I mean his stories will be told for generations to come forever probably." He mouthed a very exaggerated wow while looking at everyone.

All of them were jammed very uncomfortably into this wooden cage and they had been given no food and very little water and sat balled up next to each other and could barely move.

"I can't wait to hear what he did back there. I mean there was a volcano there once, right? We were a good hour's ride away when it happened, and we got knocked off our horses. This guy was epic no doubt. I am so sorry I missed him. Please, what was he like?"

"He was kind," said Mary,

"That volcano erupted and to save us he gave his life," said Duncan.

"He….," Amina started but the Duke cut her off. "BORING! Really, I had hoped he was a true badass. Just not enough of us these days. Well, I assure you little girl I am not nice, I embrace evil! I don't know why more people don't try it really." His face lit up as he continued.

"You get to scream at people and kill them oh and torture them, I mean the fun never stops really," he said with a huge smile. "Good night boys and girls," and he walked off back to his tent.

"What are we going to do? This guy is crazy!" said Divya, worry etched all across her face.

"We just must keep our heads and wait for the one slip up and take advantage, so we must be sharp to see it," Duncan responds.

It would take two more grueling days before they arrived at the Duke's castle. As the cart pulls up on the bridge before entry, the Duke walks up and points to the castle with both his hands, "So this is home, I can't wait to show our special brand of hospitality. I just want you to know going into this that I'm fully committed to being the very best villain I can be. I hope you appreciate all the hard work I've put into this. I mean if you're going live a life of pain and torture you want the best, a true professional. Right? Not some half-assed bad guy whose heart just really is not in it. So, in short Welcome!" he said with great joy and turned to his guards. "Now, show these good people their cell," and he walks off.

After they are put in a cell together the door shuts behind them and they all wait there in the pitch-black cell. Mary broke the silence just to ask for the 100th time, "Brewst can you feel Zen?"

"No Mary, I'm sorry, I can't feel anything," he replies again.

After a while, they saw that the only light coming from the crack in the door had gone out. Brewst put his head against the door, "I don't feel any magic near. Maybe they left."

"I found this little piece of metal," said Duncan. "Let me see if I can get the lock." He got down to his knees to try and pop the lock in the door. Occasionally, it made a slight metallic sound, and they would all go "Shhh" fearful that someone may hear them and spoil their escape plan.

"They are going hear!" Each one takes a turn saying to him. "Ok, ok I can't see, I'm doing my best," Duncan says.

After playing with it for 30 mins he finally pops the lock and Duncan says, "Half-assed bad guy," with a smirk. "Come on," he said in a low whisper and slowly they filed out and down the hall to a staircase. Divya asks Brewst, "Do you feel anyone?"

"It's hard. They are in the building but I don't think they are close. I never used my power that way before."

Slowly Duncan leads them down the stairs, the door to the level below is locked and each door till they get to the bottom. That door is unlocked, Duncan turns to the group, "Listen I think we are on the ground floor and I think this door leads to the courtyard. If you don't see anyone take off and don't stop for anything. Brewst and I will try to run interference to help you ladies get a clear path. That might mean leaving us behind, but you must keep going," Duncan instructed. He turned to the door and pulled it open. It started to make a creaky sound and Duncan stopped. He then tried opening it again, this time slower and more carefully. Finally, it was open, and he ushered the girls out and then they started to make their way across what seemed a large room, it was so dark it couldn't have been the courtyard, but there was no stopping now they pushed through. Suddenly a huge halo of light turned on near the ceiling lighting up the room and illuminating the duke sitting on his throne. He threw his hands out and shouted, "Surprise!!" He was perched on a throne at the furthest end of the room and at least 100 men surrounded them.

Laughing he said, "You should have seen the look on your face. That was a riot, come on, admit it. I saw glimmers of hope in those eyes. I love that prank," he said nearly jumping with joy. "It gets me every time, give them hope to break out and take it away. See what I told you, I'm here to give you the full experience," he said grinning from ear to ear. Then brought both his palms together in a loud clap, jumped off his throne, and came toward them

"So, this is my throne room and of course my throne. I love to say that word, it sounds tough. And I know what you're thinking, not enough skulls on it, I said the same thing myself. Can you get enough of a good thing, I'm not sure but my people here wanted me to tone the whole death thing down, so I try. So, are you wondering why I have all my men here, surely, I didn't think you were that dangerous did I? he asked with a smirk.

"It's really because now we are going to strip you all down in front of all of them. because... well it's just humiliating! Wow will you look at all these hot young bodies, yikes this is going be fun," the Duke revels in excitement.

Then some men brought in buckets of cold water and poured it over each of them as the Duke had made them stand frozen and some of the men washed them down in front of everyone to add to the humiliation.

"Now please take them down to my personal dungeon and set them up as I like it you rascal," the Duke instructs one of the men to his right.

The Duke waited an hour to let them settle in and then came into the dungeon. To the left Mary and Divya were chained to the wall with chains running to their wrists and feet which are also chained together. In the back, both guys were tied to racks face out and poor Amina was tied to a large wooden horse with her arms and legs over the sides and ropes tying her down, unable to move her limbs.

"WHOA, I have to say a tear is coming to my eye, I mean this is special. I rarely get to torture such young beautiful people and a group that love each other. Takes my breath away, I mean really, I promise I'm going to always cherish this. I hope you can too," he said sincerely.

"You know you see it all the time, the half-assed bad guy captures their prey and locks them up to rot in a dirty cell, then some stupid public execution. LAME! NO! Strip them off their dignity first I say and then break their spirits. That is what you really want from your villain and that is what you're getting from me!"

He walked up to the two men and began inspecting them as if they were horses he intended to buy. "Not bad boys," he jeered looking at their crotches, "but I really don't fancy boys. I do have a couple of extremely large guards who can't get enough though.... Hmmm that will be fun to watch," he said as he ran his hand down Duncan's stomach. "But I think we must take the fight out of you first. I think the first thing we will do is cut your balls off in front of the ladies."

"You sick, dirty bastard!" Duncan yelled.

"Really? Is that the best you got? No imagination. That is the problem with today's youth," he said giggling and getting in Duncan's face. "I guarantee when we are cutting that sack and clipping those nuts, you will come up with some much better insults. Come on, I'm trying to give my best, it's the least you can do."

"You're insane!" Duncan snapped back.

"Me?" asked the duke pointing to himself and looking around dramatically.

"You all are the ones that are insane. Trying to be good and suffering and losing all the time in the hope god will come and pat you on the butt and say 'Good dog'. What a waste of a life when you could fill it with murder and torture and break the human spirit. Now those are great achievements." He said proudly.

"I mean, do you realize how much you must rape someone before they break? It is a lot of work!" he was grinning as he said it.

Then he walked behind Amina, "Oh my sweet Dark Horse, I will truly love breaking you in." He groped her bare backside and then he ran his hand down the length of her crotch back and forth. "I wonder if you will get wet for me my darling. Oh, I am excited and I have proof," he said with glee pointing down and smiling.

"Then you two lovelies, soft and ripe."

He walks over and reaches out his hands and squeezes one of each of their breasts. Flicking their nipples. "So soft. But I must admit I'm a bit addicted to my process, so I always soften the women up with some whipping. You don't know pain till you get hit by the crack of a horsewhip. 50 lashes, and then we bring in a few of the guys to make sure those holes get stretched." He breathes in deep to savor the moment as he does Mary, who had been trying not to think about what happened to her in the past, loses control. This was all too much, and she started crying and trembling and lost control of her bladder. As he was enjoying the moment, he heard her urine hitting the cold stone floor and looked at her.

"Oh, baby you get me!" The duke said as he got close and licked the side of her face.

"Okay. This is the best part. The anticipation, truly nothing like it. So, first thing tomorrow we cut the guys' balls off and whip the two younger ones. Don't worry my sweet dark horse, you will have a great view of it all." And he strode out of the room triumphantly, slowly repeating the word, "Anticipation" in a small sort of song.

Chapter 20

A few days back:

Zen wakes up and slowly sits up and looks around. He is in a field miles away from the blast. The shock wave hit him hard, carrying him all the way to this large field. He got to his feet and looked around but didn't see a volcano, not even in the distance.

Did it work? He was not completely sure, and his head hurt a lot, so things were still very fuzzy. Suddenly he heard a voice from behind him.

"Who are you?" a disembodied voice asks. The same voice he had heard outside the city. Then two large red glowing eyes appeared 20 ft above him.

"You! How dare you? That volcano was sacred to a few gods. How dare you destroy their sacred belonging?"

This time Zen saw the punch coming and on instinct brought himself to the void but on the wall of the void you could see the red-outlined fist getting closer he shattered the walls and punched Zen out of the void and his body cartwheeled like a rag doll at least a 100 ft and he landed in a swamp. He tried to stand up, he wondered if he could do his blast again, he didn't know how or if he had done it before but before he could do anything, the being was on top of him and slammed his fist down and drove Zen into the swamp mud like a nail.

"Serves you right worm! Back to the dirt for you!" it said in its unnaturally deep voice. The spirit starts to turn and leave the swamp but the swamp starts boiling and Zen rises out of the mud and hovers over it wiping the mud from his face.

"I'm in no mood false god," Zen shouts.

"What did you say?"

Then a very dark cloud came overhead and it started to rain extremely hard. Zen held his hands up and called all the lighting down from the sky. 100s of strikes land right on the top of the being's head causing him to dematerialize. Zen fell back into the swamp and lay there completely drained and unconscious face up. The fight left him exhausted to the very core

An old -man who was born in a village in the shadows of the Great Wall in the far east was riding a cart when he watched Zen blow the volcano off the map from a distant mountain and then watched the small fight. When it was over, he came down. He stopped next to Cat, "Who threw out a perfectly good lycanthrope away? Kids these days what a waste!" he said as he used his stick as leverage to lift Cat on his cart and headed for home. As he was passing the swamp to get to his place, he watched Zen fall from the sky and drop to the ground.

"Is it raining white people, today?" He grumbled as he got off his cart and dragged Zen to the cart, threw him on top of Cat, and kept on to his house.

While Zen was out, he had terrible dreams that he killed and melted his friends. He would just dream repeatedly of all the different terrible ways that he had killed Mary and his family.

Two days later early in the morning, Zen jumped straight out of bed and ready to fight, scaring the old man.

"What Is the matter with you? I am a million years old. You're going give me a heart attack!" snaps the old man.

"Where am I? I must find my friends; do you know what happened? Where are we? How did I get here? Zen asked one question after the other.

"Asking me a million questions in a row is not going to help you at all," snapped the old man.

"Have some soup! It is good I make it myself. Of course, I make it, I'm the only asshole out here," he muttered under his breath. Zen getting flustered starts to leave and opens the door but the old man stops him, "Are you just going to leave your friend?"

"What?"

"Your friend, that giant lycanthrope lying over there. he's not with you?" he asked agitatedly.

"What do you mean lycanthrope? Do you mean Cat?" and as he said it saw huge feet peeking from under the blanket. He pulls the blanket back to find Cat lying there unconscious.

Zen turns to the old man sits down and says, "Please help me if he is …" not finishing that sentence. "People I love were with him and are now probably in danger," Zen pleaded.

"Probably, no! They are definitely, in danger and likely to be killed soon," he snapped again.

Zen sitting looked scared not knowing where Mary was.

"Does none of this seem familiar? Any of it?" the old man asked.

"That good-for-nothing spirit is just failing at his job lately," he says under his breath.

"You're the healer, you're the 5th person I'm supposed to meet," Zen remembers.

"Now think about that! You get the healer fifth! How much easier would it have been to have me along the whole time? I mean you blew a part of the planet off and shot yourself three miles backward in the process then fought a huge spirit and you're still up in two days ready to go and don't you forget it because of who!"

"Thank you, but I've lost," he said tearing up and his voice cracking. He felt and looked dejected.

The old man interjects, "What are you going to do about it Master of Elements?"

"What can I do? I don't even know where they are."

"Duke Mortiz took them, it's a three-day journey to his castle from here, and they left three days ago so you have maybe the day left to save them. He will play with them the first night, but they will all be dead a few hours after daybreak the next day. He talks a big game, but he gets flustered and suffers from performance anxiety while playing with his prey, kills them early, and spoils his fun." He said as if he had memorized Mortiz's pattern by heart.

He looked at Zen and felt a pang of guilt at the look on his face. "I'm sure you could have done without the commentary, I'm sorry."

"I have no horse and your old donkey is not the answer and I can't carry Cat, there is no way I can make it," Zen's mind was already racing with thoughts on how to save his family.

The old man drops his soup disgusted. "You are looking at my face and telling me that you, the guy who just blew a mountain off the goddam face of the planet; YOU, are crying about not having a horse and not being able to carry your friend. You don't know what to do? I will tell you what... the youth of today. I give up!."

Flustered, he points at Zen, "If I had your power my fist would already be so far up the duke's ass id be pulling on his tonsils." Zen looked confused. The old man just rolled his eyes. "Tell me you have no idea what tonsils are... go ahead," he said in a huff.

"And while we are on the topic of our grand hero being a dumb ass why did you never tell your Giant he is a lycanthrope?"

At this point, Zen was truly confused. "What? I found him in the sewers."

"That's no excuse. Has he roared much? Covered in hair?" he asked. When Zen didn't respond, the old man threw his hands in the air and huffed.

"Clueless! I tell you this boy is clueless." He said looking upward. "In one hour your non-lycanthrope friend," he said rolling his eyes, "will be healed. It just takes a bit longer as he doesn't have your power but when it comes to healing, I am pretty great. So, you have an hour to figure out how are you going to save your family, save the girl you love cause the Duke is a fate worse than death."

A couple of hours later the old man and Cat were standing outside the little hut, watching Zen trying to practice his new skill. The more he tried the more he failed, and you could see the anger, sadness, and worry building in him. After one particularly terrible failure, He got up kicked a bucket, and looked up and his eyes were glowing bright red!

It scared Cat and he stared at Zen with a shocked face, even the old man was worried. He walked over to Zen and put both of his hands on his shoulder. "Kid, you have more power than any human in history, maybe any 10 people. But absolute power corrupts absolutely, don't lose yourself to hate and rage. That is not how you got here. Use your heart, yes, but the good side of it."

At that moment the old man turned and snapped at Cat "You have been practicing for hours and nothing. What are you doing?"

Cat said, "I don't know how to; I need you to help me do it!"

"Will I need to come in and wipe your ass later also?" the old man said roughly. "Just imagine that your friends are being tortured and killed and you completely failed them."

His words were harsh and Cat looked down to the ground, helpless, dejected, and humiliated.

"I'm sorry, I'm too old, I have no people skills but take that feeling right now and let it all out. But be careful what you let out. You saw his eyes! Whatever you let out right now, it might not go back in." After coming up with the plan with the old man and trying to master their new skills they are finally ready to go. Cat looks over and says, "Thank you" and Zen follows suit.

"Are you coming with us?" Cat asks.

"I'm old, what am I going to do pee my pants to distract them, no you guys go and have a nice time. Afterwards, you know where I will be when you need me."

Chapter 21

The two girls were still crying, Duncan looked over at Brewst, "What are we going to do? No one is coming, they are all dead."

"We will have to endure and wait for our moment then make them pay," Brewst replies.

Amina says, "I can't say I find comfort in that, but I know we have no choice."

Brewst pops his head up, "I feel something."

Mary immediately asked, "Is it Zen?"

"No, I'm sorry Mary, this is not Zen. It's rage, power, and hate I've never felt anything like it, ever and it is coming here at a tremendous speed."

"Well, whatever it is maybe it will be a mercy and kill us before morning," Duncan says. Moments later they heard faint bells ringing off in the distance.

"They might not be here for us, but maybe we all won't see morning," says Amina.

After the Duke left them in his personal dungeon, he went up to his library which also happens to be the level where the top of the castle walls is. While he is looking in one of his books for different types of torture, in hopes of finding something new. He hears extremely heavy rain start to come down and hears it hitting the windows. "Wow! That storm came out of nowhere," he thought aloud when he heard the guards on the wall top screaming and making a commotion. So, he walks out, and his eyes are drawn up as he sees the guards staring up.

When lightning struck, lighting up the sky as they streaked across the sky and hit the outstretched hands of a man floating about 50 ft above them. "Absolute LEGEND!" the Duke screams as his jaw drops

"This guy lives up to the hype, I mean goddam could that have been cooler?" he was thinking as Zen projected his voice down.

"Give them to me or I will tear you and this castle apart piece by piece!"

By now the Duke was jumping up and down with joy, "And voice projection on top of it, what a time to be alive," the Duke said to himself, and he ran back into the building and tried to hurriedly get dressed for a fight. By that time the bells had rung, and all the men had filed out to the courtyard. The Duke comes out in his disheveled armor and stands behind them.

"Very cool light show but you're too late I already had them skinned," the Duke yelled.

Zen's eyes begin to glow red again, he stretches his arm forward and built-up lightning comes out and vaporizes the first couple of guys. Then he makes a fist with his right hand and points it at a man in the front and the man starts violently shaking faster and faster till he pops, and his inside and fluids fly everywhere.

Zen then starts pointing both fists at people and they start popping which sends the crowd into a frenzy to get out of the courtyard. As he keeps targeting people, his whole body starts glowing with a dark red aura around him casting a strange light in the now completely dark night sky as the rain poured down.

Cat, who had been waiting for the signal that never came watched in horror. Zen seemed to be transforming into something much darker. So, Cat ran toward the door and a warrior monk who had been hiding came out of nowhere and stabbed Cat in the stomach, making him fall to one knee. The monk pulled out his sword and Cat fell to the ground, and he pulled back the sword to make the final blow and all Cat could think of was what the old man had said.

'Just imagine that your friends are being tortured and killed and you completely failed them.' The old man's words kept ringing in his ears.

As the sword came down Cat let out one last roar but this one was full of pain, loss, and failure. It was so loud it distracted Zen. For a moment he came back to his senses and looked for Cat and didn't notice that above the castle wall to his right now stood two very large glowing red eyes.

"YOUUUUU!" The deep voice said and shook the castle walls as he said it.

Zen then quickly turns.

"The disrespect you show worm will not be tolerated," said the eyes as the giant threw a right-handed punch that landed right on Zen's face which sent him flying cartwheel style through the air. As he was flying, he heard Cat roar once more, but this time was different than all the rest.

As the sword comes down, Cat blocks it with his arm which cuts halfway into it and Cat looks him dead in the face. He roars and turns into the monster of men's nightmares. His skin hardened and claws ripped through his hands and his eyes turned dark purple. He punched straight through the monk's chest and threw him off his arm. He stood up, pulled the sword out of his arm, and roared again.

"Is that Cat?" Divya asks between sniffling as they faintly hear Cat's roars.

"No, that sounds like something else," Duncan says.

"Guys, when I feel the Duke's power it is dark and slippery but whatever is up there feels like pure hate," he said looking up to the ceiling.

Zen flies around trading strikes with the being, hitting him with lightning and stones that have fallen off the walls. Zen's being much faster than the giant helped but when it managed to connect with Zen, he really had no defense against it, and that made him angrier. At the same time, Zen is also fending off acts from the warrior monks below.

He stands still for a moment hoping he can dematerialize the Giant again, but it screams and is ready for the attack this time. It blows a stream of fire straight at Zen which is a direct shot and Zen falls backward to the ground with his hair and skin completely burnt off.

The Duke and his men are just awe-struck and just standing there watching the blows being traded. Zen just lay there trying to pull himself together before the giant being put his fists together and drove them down on Zen's body.

Back in the dungeon they keep hearing these roars, screams, and explosions and can't help but think the worst, maybe some enemy of the Duke had come to get revenge. It seemed very plausible.

Just as Brewst was thinking that he had heard Cat's roar, a boom ensued blocking that chain of thought. He really thought this was the end. He said, " I just want you all to know that I love you guys!"

Everyone voiced their replies. Something hit the large iron door hard and then again. All of them stare scared at the door, and suddenly the door is ripped out of the wall. The entire door and jam are thrown down the hall as this creature screams again and in walks a tall silver-haired giant.

Amina yells "Cat?"

Cat's still stuck in savage mode so he roars again but this time you can hear the relief in it.

Clearing his voice, "Yes, it's me." As he stood triumphantly in the doorway happy he found them. He had to beat and kill many of the Duke's men to get them to show the way to where they were.

"How?" they all asked at once.

"No time we got to get out of here now."

The girls yelled, "Yes, please get us out of these," waving their hands in the claps.

He pops them with his claw and bends over and pops their feet chains and over to the boys and finally rips Amina's ropes. He said as he rubbed against her to cut her ropes, "Sorry, I'm sorry.."

She jumped up and off the wooden horse and said, "I'm just happy to see you." Cat then looks down at her naked body and before can get a word out she says, "Enough, let's go!"

"What is going on up there Cat?" Divya asked.

Cat looked right at Mary and said, "It is Zen." She screamed, "He is still alive."

Cat then looks off to the side, "I'm not sure he is the Zen we knew. He is different!"

Mary not listening to that part says, "Let's go get him." They all file behind Cat and he leads them out the door and down the hall. "Wait! We need some clothes," demands Mary.

Cat runs down the hall and investigates some rooms. "You guys must wear monks' outfits that is all that's here. Ok just get the ones that will the least amount of blood please." Divya asks.

They finally make their way up to the courtyard just in time to see Zen lying on the ground and getting pounded repeatedly into the ground.

"No, they all scream!" The giant has hit Zen so hard that he has indented the ground. The giant again hits Zen with an extra-long fire stream and he lays there motionless as burnt muscle. The smell of burnt skin hangs in the air. Cat then grabs Mary, rounds up the rest, and starts heading to the front gate. Mary is putting up a fight, hanging over his shoulder reaching back to Zen screaming his name, unwilling to leave him behind. Duncan says, "It doesn't feel right leaving him." Cat says, "What the hell can we do? He would want me to make sure you all were safe."

As the giant then pulled both fists up over his head the Duke proclaimed, "This is the best night of my life!" He was not even paying attention to his prey escaping.

As they were running, they got to the gate, and all looked back at the giant coming to make the final blow when they all heard a loud clap sound. It took a second, but they saw two gold-glowing eyes now standing over Zen's body. Both red and gold giants with translucent bodies went head to head and all you can see is a red or gold outline of the bodies. And its hands had caught the red giant's fists and threw them back up and punched the red giant right in the throat. Knocking it back.

"What the hell is that?" Duncan said

"I think that is his power, his magic is protecting him!" Brewst says.

"How is it possible?" Divya yells over the fight noise.

"I have no idea, I guess it loved him so much it won't let him die," Brewst replies.

The group as well as the Duke and all his men watched mesmerized by what they were seeing.

The gold giant was tied to Zen so it could not move like the Red one but they both traded blow after blow. Due to the lack of movement, it was hard to get on top of the red one and red could dodge gold's attacks easier. The red hits the gold one with a fire attack over and over, also hitting it with an electrical attack in between. Then would try to land blows on the gold being, making its gold outline fade a bit.

Because of this, the golden giant now grabbed the arms of the red and pulled Zen's body up off the ground held it near the middle, and took off straight up. They fly so high up that no one on the ground can see the outlines anymore. The gold giant then with one arm plunges it into the middle of the red giant and snaps. A blinding burst of light!

Another mushroom cloud explosion lights up the entire night sky and radiates out for miles.

Everyone gasps even the warrior monks, the Duke stands there with tears in his eyes and says, "-- legend" quietly to himself.

It didn't take long but while the sky was still bright, they could make out a body falling to Earth. The way his legs and arms were dangling, no doubt he was unconscious. But his golden outline was nowhere to be seen and all they could do was watch. But as he got closer to the ground you could see something was slowing his fall and then finally gently put him down in the courtyard of the Duke's castle.

He lay there burnt and bleeding, missing some parts, and his shoulder and arm completely busted. Duncan yelled to Brewst, "Take the monk's powers." But he couldn't. Zen's power had now changed somehow and was masking his power but since he was between Brewst and the monks, Brewst couldn't see past him to see anyone's power at all.

Mary ran to him, and the rest followed. At that point, the Duke and his men realized they had escaped, and he yelled, "Who let them out?" And just as he was giving the order to go get them Mary reached and touched Zen who even in that state saw what happened to her and what happened in the dungeon, and his eyes turned dark red and he then floated up to a standing position but a few feet in the air and they all watched as the red aura came back and completely healed him in seconds in front of everyone.

Just then Mary grabbed his legs and thought, "Please don't give in to hate, don't be an evil spirit like me, think of a better moment."

At her words, the moment that came to mind, was of him sitting on the wall and watching them all dance being silly on the rooftop as the sun was going down. As he thought and relived that memory the silver dagger, he always wore on his belt started to glow till it lit up the entire courtyard. Zen reached down to grab the handle and that made the aura go away, and Zen dropped to his hands and knees.

He was helped to his feet by Mary. He kissed her and told them all to run and get behind the castle wall, he was too weak and was not sure he could control this. Having no idea what was coming they ran out the gate. As they were running the Duke screamed, "Get them!"

Zen turned around and all that the group saw on the other side of the wall was a greyish light that sparked for a moment and then went dark. They all ran back to find Zen alive, but sort of half burnt, and half-healed it seemed he was losing the power to heal or stay healed. And they looked over and all the warrior monks had been turned to statues as they ran toward him. However, there was no sign of the Duke.

187

Chapter 22

Mary tried to hold him the best she could and asked, "Now what?" looking up at the others as Zen lay bleeding.

"It's ok. I know what to do." Cat said as he turned back to himself but with a vicious cut into his arm and other places. They took the prisoner cart, took the top off, put Cat and Zen in it, and Cat led them back to the old man pointing out the way as Duncan and Brewst helped navigate the horses and the two girls walked behind.

Mary was sitting with Zen's head on her lap as he slowly regained consciousness looked up at her and said "Hey."

"Hi," she replied with a huge smile and a tear in her eye.

She leaned down and kissed him on his forehead trying not to move him too much with all the pain he was in.

And they made the slow journey back to the old man's place so that both could be healed for whatever might be next.

After making potions and wraps and steam heat with herbs in it the two were set in a small room the old man had dug out of the ground with a door so they could sleep and be left alone till the healing processes had taken place.

After finally finishing, the old man went back to his humble home where everyone else was cramped but happy to be safe. Mary thanked him but the old man looked into her eyes and said, "It was my great honor, my lady."

"So, you are the fifth person that was to join his party, seems to make more sense if you had been first," she said, "Would have made a lot of other things easier."

"I told him the same thing; you will need to help him with planning these things," he smiled.

"When we saw him fighting, he had red eyes and a red aura at times, what does that mean?" Mary asked.

"His powers have reached a God-like status, and they will be tied to his emotions, but he must realize hate and anger are easy ways to power. He will have to decide what sort of person he wants to be now that he is the strongest human ever. Make no mistake, he could think his righteous anger is helping when it is the complete opposite!"

After Zen was on his way to recovery, he had a dream that he was sitting in his void and thinking of his friends when a golden person showed up. "Who are you?" asked Zen.

It walked over to him and pointed to his heart.

"Are you my power, the thing inside me that makes up the power?" Zen asked.

It nodded yes.

Zen said, "Thank you for saving me and my friends, I truly love you and couldn't do anything without you." It came in closer and hugged him tightly.

When it stopped, Zen said, "You know there is no way I can pass my test now." looking down.

"I just want you to know that it's my fault, not yours, I suppose this means your life will end also but this is my fault, you just did what I asked." Then in his dream, he sat down and on the wall in the void played Zen's favorite moments the gold figure sat close next to him and leaned its head on Zen's shoulder and they both watched in silence.

After almost a week Zen and Cat were healthy again and strong enough to move so on the last night they had a feast with the old man thanking him for his part and he pretended not to love it.

At some point before the party Zen and Mary walked outside to see the stars. "I really have no idea how to say this, but I will fail my test," Zen says. "The Guide has already told me."

"WHAT!?!" Mary yells

She grabs him and holds him tight, "This is not fair I can't lose you now, I just got you back."

"I know, I know, I'm sorry but it was my choice to not be submissive with my powers and now I'm in a no-win situation." Mary just gave way to tears and pushed her face deep into Zen's chest.

"Can you run away, run and hide, use your powers so they can't find you?" Mary begged.

"It doesn't work like that my sweet, I'm sorry."

"I just wanted you to know first, no secrets on my side either," he said with a weak smile.

Mary and Zen tried to act like nothing was wrong but didn't want to spoil everyone's victory dinner.

At the end of the night, the guide showed up and told Zen it was time to tell them. He looked out and said, "After Zen destroyed a sub-god of a powerful deity, that deity has challenged to be Zen's test. It's nothing personal for this deity but he must stick up for his sub-god's or his whole line is worthless. He really has no choice but to defend his god lines honor."

"No matter how strong Zen has become there is no way he can defeat him," the guide says softly.

They all rose to their feet. "This is outrageous after all we have been through this man has saved us repeatedly," they all said shouting over each other. He allowed them to complain and act out but when they finally calmed down, he said, "Zen was warned many times to be careful about attracting too much attention and he made personal choices to disregard that order," the guide reminded them.

"To save us Guide this is terrible how can you allow it?" Brewst yelled.

"There are rules and they won't be broken," sadly the Guide pointed out.

"Is there anything you can do?" asked Mary with tears in her eyes having already been told in private by Zen.

"I have got him the full 90 days of rest before the test. We wanted to tell you now so you can all enjoy your time together."

"Can we ask what is the final test and what happens?" Duncan asks.

"Well, if he won, he could choose three outcomes; 1 - come back to earth and rule for a time as a mortal human and try to send civilization forward a bit with his power. 2 - He could decide to become a spirit being and ascend there. Or 3 - he could ask for time here but then he would have to ascend. He will have to face off against the Deity in a thing that sort of looks like the void he has taken you all to. Whichever way it goes you all will be notified. I will make sure," assured the guide.

"What would you like to do Zen?" the group inquired.

"I would like for all of us to go back to that island, it was the best time of my life. I would like to enjoy the rest of it there," Zen said.

"The Guide gave me all your wishes and I wish for all of you to find happiness and peace going forward even without me," Zen said with a weak smile.

The next day they all left and got on a boat back to the island with Hero and Cedella excitedly waiting to greet them again.

The next 90 days went fast but they all did their best to enjoy that time, Zen really had a hard time but knew each moment, especially with his Mary, was special. She was who he wanted to share his last moments with. When his last week came, Cat yelled up, "Zen you have a visitor."

He and Mary went down, and it was Machitis.

"It hurts me in a way I can't describe in your language, but I have never felt that way for a human," Marchitis said.

He turned to Mary and said, "Many years ago my son sacrificed his life to save mine and while a part of me died that day I was so very proud of him. I never got to tell him that, you all need to make sure you do since you have been given the gift of time." Machitis said.

"Sadly, it takes most beings to lose before they appreciate what they have but we need to make sure we show appreciation for those around us while we can," Machitis said with a shaky voice.

"When you get to the other side, please find my son and tell him I'm so proud of him for me and I'll see him soon," Machitis asked.

Zen said nothing, just shook his head.

And with that, Machitis left

On his last full day, they all spent some time together in the ocean and then up on the roof terrace all telling each other which moment they loved the best and reminding each other of certain parts of the adventures they had together.

As usual Zen just watched but this time held Mary as tight as he could, fully knowing he loved these people. They were his family and he was thankful they made him a better person and loved him.

On the very last night, they would be together, and everyone else left to go to bed after drinking and being in the sun all day. Mary waited for Zen to come back upstairs. She grabbed his hand and took him back to the roof and sat him on the table. She undressed him and started kissing him all over. Then she stood back and slowly took her dress off in front of him doing a cute little spin and dance. She was so pretty and self-conscious which made it all so much more adorable. It was hard for Zen because he could feel the overwhelming sadness in her but she wanted tonight to be special and about him. She poured her whole heart into giving him as much pleasure as she could but could not help crying while they made love. Then they lay there afterwards staring back up at the stars like the first time. It felt as if it was just the two of them in the world. Tomorrow's worries are nonexistent at this moment.

Zen turned and said, "I love you, thank you for everything, you were the best part!"

She smiled cuddled up against him and said I know.

On the last day, the Guide came to get him and Zen handed a letter to Brewst, one to Duncan, and then one to Mary but said, "Don't open it till you bury me." Zen said, "It's always easier to leave but I'm sad I'm leaving you all behind." Kissed Mary and told her he loved her.

Then just like that they were both gone. It was very hard on everyone in different ways. After the Guide and Zen disappeared they all stood there shocked for a while. Not knowing what to do. Hero made everyone something to eat but this time they all sat in silence thinking about Zen. After which the guys opened their letters and read them aloud to share what it said with the rest of the group.

After he left the two men opened their letters

Dear Brewst

Thank you for your friendship and I'm glad you didn't leave the group. After this is all done, please take Divya and Amina back to see the high wizard. I had him give me four rooms in his personal cellar. I told him the fourth was for Mary, but it was for him. I have filled them with gold and want the four of you to each have one of the rooms. I know Amedeo is already rich and powerful, but I want to thank him. Enjoy life just as you always have, and I hope this is the beginning of your next adventure.

Your friend,

Zen

Man of few words Brewst thought.

Dear Duncan

You're the best and I will miss you terribly. When this is over, please take Cat and Mary to Akhenaten's place and tell Gregnow I won't be making it. Let Mary have the house and bury me in the garden with Akhenaten and his wife. There is a huge treasure vault under the house that took Akhenaten 3000 years to fill please split it four ways for all of you and Gregnow. Please be there for Mary and tell Cat he is there to protect her. I'm sure they will understand when you tell them you must go back to Cedella.

Your friend,

Zen

The Guide stands next to Zen at the beginning of a long very extremely large bright white hallway. "It was fun watching you work Zen, I'm sorry it went this way."

"Me too," Zen replied.

Chapter 23

"I have helped many different species through their life and journeys, but I have to say Zen you have achieved many great things but maybe the best was the amount of love and friendships you had in your life. I do think that is how one has a good life. You truly proved yourself worthy of the gifts you have been given."

Zen looked at his friend with a smile and said nothing, just looked away and then looked back and reached out his hand and said, "Thank you, my friend, thank you for your guidance."

Then they both nodded to each other, and Zen started to walk down the large hallway. Of course, it is there to intimidate but it is also a metaphor for how large his competitor is as the hallway is 100 feet tall and 100 feet wide but 1000 feet long all shiny white marble. The only sound was that of Zen's boots tapping on the white marble floor as he walked to the door.

As he took the long walk, he couldn't help but wonder what Mary was doing at that moment. He would not let himself think of his friends being sad at that moment, just happy thoughts he tried. He saw Mary reading a book on the roof terrace one fall evening in the future to Cat sitting on the ground with his grave in the background. It made him happy, not that it was his grave, but they were all there together.

Maybe Brewst and Divya would go on great adventures together and bring Amina along for protection. That made him giggle. I could see Duncan holding Cedella at the house on the island taking care of Hero.

No matter what happened to him next, he won that, that was a success no doubt about it.

As he gets closer to the door, he sees that it is already open a crack which is way more than enough room for him but that there is also a figure standing there at the door. He is hoping it is Mary standing there one last time, as a small parting gift from the Guide maybe. But as he gets closer, he sees who it is. "Come to see me off hey?" Zen asks.

"I'm sorry son, this is a terrible deal," says the old man as he puts his hands one on his chest and the other on his back, and as he rubs a white circle of light shows up around his hands. After which he says, "Here is your 5th object," and hands him a wooden staff with a volcanic rock base perched on top. The rock floats just above the top of the staff. Red and purple colored electrical arches surround the stone. The staff appears to hold immense power.

"Thanks! But I don't think it is of any use now." Zen says dejectedly, and as he starts to walk forward the old man grabs his arm.

"Now wait a God Damn minute, you are telling me the guy who blew a mountain off the face of the planet is defeated. The man who can fly? The man who blew apart the asshole sub-god? Who speeds up aging? Who just happens to make an extra hot body for the girl he would just happen to fall in love with? The God damn master of elements is coming, and this idiot has no idea what he is in for! I want you to go in there and kick this jerk's ass." He slaps him on the butt and pushes him toward the door opening.

197

Zen giggles shaking his head and says nothing to it. Holds up his staff, thanks the old man and says, "Hey, I never caught your name."

"I'll tell you the next time we meet," the old man says with a huge smile and a wink.

Zen smiled, bowed to him, and then turned to continue his journey. He walks in through the large doorway and steps into the light.

Made in the USA
Monee, IL
24 November 2023

47194194R00116

ISBN 9781962568166

9 781962 568166